FOXCRAFT

FOXCRAFT

⭑BOOK ONE⭑
THE TAKEN

Foxc

BOOK ONE
THE TAKEN

FOXCRAFT

BY
INBALI ISERLES

 SCHOLASTIC PRESS / NEW YORK

Library of Congress Cataloging-in-Publication Data Available

ISBN 978-0-545-69081-2

10 9 8 7 6 5 4 3 2 1   15 16 17 18 19

Printed in the U.S.A. 23
First edition, October 2015
Book design by Nina Goffi

FOR AMITAI FRASER ISERLES,
OUR LITTLE FOX.

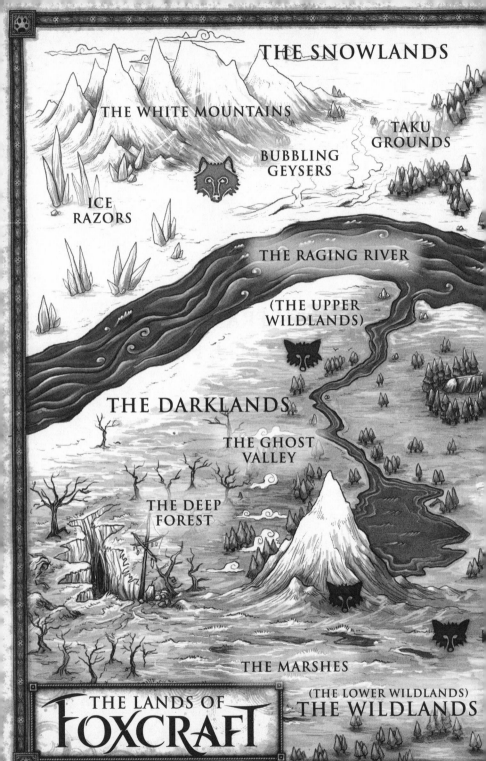

GROWL
WOOD

TO THE SEA

THE WILDLANDS

THE ELDER
ROCK

THE FREE LANDS

THE WILDWAY

THE BEAST
DENS

THE GRAYLANDS
(THE GREAT SNARL)

ISLA'S
DEN

THE DEATHWAY

Blando

1

My paws slipped on dry earth. I kicked up shrouds of dust as I hurtled toward the fence. Swerving to avoid it, I righted myself and dived under the splintering dead wood. My pursuer was gaining on me as I grasped for the wildway, the tangle of greenery on the other side. I caught the rich aroma of hazel and cedar, the quiet and peace of the world beyond the web of grass.

His shrill cry shattered the silence.

With a surge of panic, I squeezed beneath the fence. Clods of soil clasped at my belly, tugging me back. My heart thundered in my ears. For an instant the dead wood enclosed me, pinning me to the earth. The grass mocked me, tickling my whiskers.

With a desperate shake I was free, lost in the green maze of the wildway.

Stooping snowdrops bobbed on their stems, snaps of white light.

I held my breath.

A pointed snout poked under the fence, stabbing the air. The fox's amber eyes caught mine, the black slits narrowed. Fear murmured at the back of my neck. I calmed myself; I was safe: he was too large to shuffle beneath the fence. He smacked against it with a growl, his slender black foreleg reaching through the gap, his claws grazing the earth by my paw.

I reared back, keeping my eyes on the fence. He couldn't go any further. He knew it too; he drew himself away, his leg disappearing behind the fence. I could hear him pacing. Flashes of his mottled red coat were visible each time he passed the gap. Then he disappeared from view and grew quiet. I was quiet too, inhaling the air.

I sensed the fox. The shape of his body. The silver-and-gold dappled brush of his tail. I pictured the color in the eye of my mind and felt the bristles of his tail hairs as though I was touching them. For an instant, I saw the far side of the fence and tasted the frustration that tingled on his tongue.

I knew this fox like my shadow.

My ear rotated. A bird was cawing in a nearby tree. It was large, its feathers glossy black, and it paused when it spotted me. It dipped its beak, stepping nervously from foot to foot. Then it arched its shimmering wings as though summoning storm clouds. With an angry caw it rose in the sky.

Wood shrieked and I spun round, my heart lunging against my chest. He had thrown himself at the gap! He burst through in a shower of wood chips. My stomach clenched and I bolted, plunging through the grass. I threw a look over my shoulder and saw him, for an instant, as he hunkered down to the ground.

In a flicker the fox vanished before my eyes.

The air in his wake had a gossamer sheen, like light bent through the wings of bees. The earth was a blur of grass and soil.

I knew his tricks and blinked furiously, catching a flash of his pelt. I rounded a tree stump in a flurry of grass. When I glanced back again he was in plain sight, his fur a blaze of red as he vaulted the stump. His breath was at the tip of my brush.

But I had a trick of my own.

I threw open my jaws and cawed like the bird with the shimmering feathers. I cast my voice to the twisted tails of the grass stems, to the fence, and the earth, and the clouds that gathered at the edges of the sky, mimicking the creature as best I could.

I zigzagged through grass that snaked around my paws, pulling and beckoning, slowing me down. I gave it up: the cawing—it wouldn't fool anyone.

I snuck another look over my shoulder. He was danger-ously close now, his muzzle at my heels.

"Pirie!" I yelped as he pounced at me and his claws glanced my brush. I might have known that the birdcall wouldn't stop him. I turned to face him, baring my teeth. "Enough!" I hissed.

His eyes caught the light. "Not till you beg for mercy!"

I started to run again, but with a final leap he slammed his paws on my back and threw me to the ground. I bucked against his grip, but he was stronger than me. "Mercy!" he gasped. "Say it!"

"Never!" I spat.

He pressed his muzzle to my ear. "Say it! Say it or else!"

"Or else what?"

"Or else this!" He dropped on top of me, covering my face with long lashes of his tongue, licking my ears, my nose, my whiskers.

I growled and licked my brother back, tickling his belly till he whimpered and twisted away, rolling in the dirt as I swiped at his neck. "You see, there is no 'or else'! You may be bigger than me, but I'm cleverer. And I *always* win!"

He allowed me to assault him with gentle nips. "I let you win," he panted. "I know what a bad loser you are."

"You're dreaming." I clambered to my paws and shook off my fur.

Pirie looked up at me, his head cocked. "Whatever you say, little fox," he gekkered mischievously—a series of high-pitched, stuttering clicks. "Mad fox, bad fox, just another dead fox!" It was something we often chanted together, though Greatma complained it set her hairs on end.

"I'm not that much smaller than you!" I scowled.

He hopped, skipped, and turned on the spot with a cheerful *wow-wow-wow*. "Little fox, little fox, you'll always be the little fox!"

I sprang at him, but he ducked out of the way.

"And you'll always be my foolish brother," I sniffed.

He looped back to me, pressing the white of his muzzle against my neck. The game was over. I didn't fight him anymore. I closed my eyes and let the warmth of his body seep into mine. I could feel his pulse against my jaw. My own seemed to fall into step with it. We ran to the same *ka-thump, ka-thump*, growing slower now, *kaa-thump, kaa-thump*.

Fa stepped out from between the tall grass. "I hope you're playing nicely together, foxlings."

Ma appeared beside him. "Nicely?" Her eyes twinkled.

We hurried toward them, panting as they licked our ears, clicking and warbling.

"We're *always* nice," yipped Pirie, throwing me a look. Ma seemed ready to question this but stopped when Greatma approached. Like Pirie, her fur was mottled in thick hairs of silver, ginger, and gold that glistened in the light. Her eyes were watchful, and she seemed distracted when we ran to her.

"The furless?" Fa watched her face for clues.

We stared over the tall grass. The wildway was a narrow area, little more than a path of green between gray territories, dotted with a few young trees.

The two-legged furless rarely entered here, but they were always close, baying, pacing, beating out the tempo of their noisy lives. The Great Snarl was their world, forbidden to young foxes: a rigid land of towering buildings and manglers with unblinking eyes. Snatchers stalked when the sun was up, furless with sticks who rounded up foxes that were never seen again.

Greatma pulled her gaze away. "It was nothing." She lowered her muzzle and touched our noses. "You play so rough, you two. Pirie, you're larger than Isla. I hope you remember that."

"She's tough as dried rat's skin," he sniffed, giving me a friendly shove.

Greatma's snout crinkled. "All the same . . ."

"I can hold my own," I piped up. "Mad fox, bad fox—"

"Stop that," growled Greatma. "The Snarl is dangerous. You shouldn't joke about it."

Pirie moved quickly to lighten the mood. "Isla's birdcall really threw me," he told Greatma.

She cocked her head to watch me more closely. "Were you imitating a crow?"

My brush thumped the grassy earth. I was more interested in what Pirie was saying. "It really worked?"

Pirie panted cheerfully. "I didn't think it was your voice at all. It was coming from nowhere and everywhere. It was . . ." One of his downy black ears flipped back. "It was like the wind was calling, and the earth, and the grass. I didn't know where I was! Then the birdcall stopped and I realized it was you."

I tipped my head and watched him. Was he teasing me? "But it didn't fool you . . ." My voice came out a whine and my ears were flat.

"You should have kept it up. You're getting too good at that, little fox!" He nuzzled my shoulder and I nipped him gently.

"You both have fine instincts," said Greatma, a hint of pride in her voice. She lifted her snout and her face grew still. Her eyes stared unblinking, the tensing of whiskers her only movement. "A breeze is rising," she murmured. "It is touched with river and ice. The rain will be here by first light."

"But the air is warm!" I blurted out.

Ma stepped closer, her ears twisting so they pointed out to the sides. "What simple lesson can save a fox's life?"

Pirie and I spoke together: "Watch! Wait! Listen!"

The tension eased on Greatma's face and she looked at us with affection. "That's right, foxlings. Watch, wait, listen . . . The answers are written in the song of the sky and the rhythm of the earth." She raised her muzzle and sniffed again.

I mimicked her, inhaling the fragrance of grass and soil. I sensed no dampness, only the mild air of the deep sun. The clouds fringing the sky were white. I blinked at them, remembering from Greatma's teachings that only the dark ones were heavy with rain. She must have caught the confusion in my face, as she gave my nose a reassuring lick.

Fa trod next to us. "We should move the kill. It's in a shallow cache. The rain will spoil it."

Fa and Ma started toward the fence. Greatma trailed behind them, throwing a quick, anxious glance into the sky. They were too big to crawl under the gap where the wood was broken—even where Pirie had burst through and made it larger. They skirted along the edge of the wildway to the far side of the fence. There was a tree there with a drooping branch that bridged our patch. Pirie knew about this tree, just as I did—we'd wobbled along the branch many times. But he'd never have used it during our chase. Play had rules—we both understood that.

"Come on," called Ma.

I wasn't ready to leave. There was a sweetness in the air. Were berries hidden in the tangle of grass? I licked my chops.

Pirie was busy with a stick, rolling it in the grass and gnawing on it like a bone.

I sat, ears flattened. "We only just got to the wildway!"

Fa called over his shoulder. "We'll come back later. Pirie? Isla?"

Pirie turned to follow them, abandoning the stick.

I rose to my paws. A deep sniff and I was certain there were berries. If I gathered a few and took them back to the den, the others would be pleased. And if I was quick, I'd still be there before them—Ma, Fa, and Greatma had to move the kill.

Crouched down, slipping between the long grasses, I followed my nose. I shivered with pleasure, absorbing the aroma of earth and bark, the sour tang of leaves and insects in their bitter shells. I paused to tear off some snowdrops, which always looked better than they tasted. A large green beetle scuttled along the soil and I batted at it excitedly, tearing grass with a sweep of my claws. The beetle was quicker than it looked. It scurried toward the base of a tree where it was hard to reach, nosing its way between bucking roots. I plunged my snout into the soil, snapping and yipping, but instead of the beetle I brought up a mouthful of dirt. *Forget the beetle!* I told myself, my thoughts returning to berries. I sniffed and prowled around the wildway, but the sweet scent had faded. There was a new chill in the air that made me remember Greatma's warning of rain . . .

Of a breeze touched with river and ice.

I looked to the sky. Darkness was creeping over jagged gray buildings. The sun slunk low, trailing a crimson light. I turned back toward the fence with a guilty skip of the heart. Ma and Fa would be worried about me. I was not allowed on my own in the wildway—was not even supposed to leave our patch without Pirie.

I retraced my steps to the fence and crawled underneath.

Our patch lay to the far side of the fence. It was a space we shared with the furless, though we were careful to avoid it when they were out. Like us, only one family used it—two adults, two young. Fa had warned us that they wouldn't be friendly, that they'd turn on us if we came too close.

We kept our distance.

Our den was set away from theirs, behind a copse not far from the fence. I gamboled toward it, thinking of the cache. Ma, Fa, and Greatma would have dug out those juicy rats they'd caught last night. My belly growled and I picked up speed.

A bitter smell seized my nose. I saw flares of red light amid the darkness of the den. Smoke spun in slow plumes, murky against the last fizzle of sun.

A ripple of fear ran along my back.

Where is my family?

I didn't sense them.

I took a step closer. There was movement in the den. My chest unclenched and I bounded forward, that instant of confusion gone. Then my pawsteps faltered and the blood drained from my body.

The things that were moving in there—I could tell it wasn't them. It wasn't my family.

I backed into a cluster of ivy that hung off the fence, not far from the gap that led to the wildway. The den was a trench by the trunk of a tree, hidden beyond the copse amid fallen branches. It was hard to see what was going on in there. I could just make out the shapes of unfamiliar foxes, maybe five or six, creeping about, digging and yelping to each other. What were they doing? Didn't the smoldering earth singe their paws? I squeezed deeper behind the ivy, holding my breath as they climbed, one by one, from the den.

They stepped onto the grass, snouts low, ears pricked. They were met by a thickset vixen who trod toward the entrance, her brush curling around her flank. From behind the tumbling ivy I could see her short, round ears and her lumbering frame. Her fur bunched at her shoulders, as though she had too much of it. She thumped a forepaw on the earth. Her ears swiveled around and the other foxes looked at her.

A growl rumbled in the vixen's throat. One gray eye glared across our patch. Where her other eye should have been, there was nothing at all—a sunken cave of darkness.

I could not control my shivering legs or the acid that stole the breath from my throat.

"Death," she hissed, and the foxes stiffened. "The Master has spoken—all traitors will die!"

The foxes rolled back onto their paws, preparing to fight. But who was there to challenge them?

Where was my bold, courageous Ma? Where were Fa's protective jaws? I thought of my brother and wise, old Greatma. *Where has my family gone?*

The vixen's lips peeled back as she snarled, revealing a row of serrated teeth.

I gasped as I shrank against the wall. It was a tiny sound, like the wings of a moth.

But the vixen froze.

Her head shot around.

Her single gray eye was gleaming with menace. It roved over the ivy and seized on me.

2

The vixen stepped nearer, a loping movement. One leg was too short, perhaps once broken. I folded in on myself, becoming as small as possible—a speck of dirt on the wooden fence. I wished I had mastered Pirie's tricks for disappearing. Had the vixen glimpsed me? Would she pick up my scent?

She paused only brush-lengths in front of me. Fear coursed through my body in sickening waves. The vixen reached out a paw and gnawed at a burr. Was it possible she hadn't seen me with that piercing gray stare?

Her whiskers twitched. "Did you say there were only four?"

A tawny fox drew next to the vixen. The rest of the strange skulk was still standing at attention, ready to pounce. The tawny fox had a slender gait. Her narrow brush dusted the ground. I noticed a strange scar near the top of her foreleg—a pattern like a broken rose, beautiful and ghastly. "The parents and the foxling son. There was a greatma too." She had a jittery voice.

I whimpered inside. *Where is my family?*

The vixen's whiskers flexed with tension. "Them and no others? Just one cub born to the ma of the den?"

The slender fox's ears pricked up. "One cub, Karka, four foxes in all. Have you reason to think—"

The vixen wheeled around and snapped at her. "I told you not to ask questions!"

The slender fox cringed. "I'm sorry," she mumbled.

That single gray eye glowered into the gathering darkness. For a moment the vixen took in the tall, square building that was the den of the furless. Light flickered through one of its large spy holes. "You never know who could be listening . . . The Elders have eyes, hooded eyes everywhere!"

My heart thundered in my chest. It was all I could do not to turn and run, back beneath the fence to the wildway. They would hear—they would catch me.

The thickset fox shook out her fur. I smelled cinder and ash. "Our enemies will not get far. Tarr is already searching. Traitors, all of them!" She slammed down her forepaw.

The other foxes threw back their heads. Their voices rose in haunting cackles. "Traitors!" they cried. "All of them, traitors!"

I huddled to the earth as the vixen turned. She began to lead the others beyond the den, loping over the fallen branch to the wildway.

I could breathe again, but only just. I hurried to the den. The embers were low, the last crackles of charcoal drifting like mist. I peered inside, taking in the ash that coated the bed of twigs. There was a patch of dappled fur there, silver and gold; I spotted a red trickle of bittersweet blood.

I stifled a cry.

My family had disappeared.

Their scent still lingered on the bark of the tree trunk, the cold, bitter earth, the twigs on the soil. I turned to stare into the yard. The light was fading fast, the dusk a gloomy pelt that swathed the world in darkness.

"Ma . . . ? Pirie . . . ?"

My ears rotated and I listened. I could hear a furless creature inside its huge den, barking in a low voice. But outside there was no reassuring yelp from my parents; no playful yips from Pirie.

Instead I heard a rustle of leaves. There was movement near the fallen branch that led to the wildway. My heart leaped with hope. The silhouette of a fox—it might be Fa! It might be—

I made out small, round ears and a lumbering frame. In the vanishing light, the single gray eye flashed green.

My blood curdled in my chest.

"A foxling! I knew it!" Suddenly she was flanked by others, who balanced along the branch to the wildway. They stormed the patch with jaws bared, howling and cackling.

I scrambled around and bolted beneath the fence into the wildway, breaking through the long grass, past the tree where the beetle had scurried to safety. My legs flew beneath me as I dived under a hedge, skidding on the ground of the other side. I was beyond the wildway, on the hard stone paths of the furless, squeezing between their legs as they stumbled in surprise. They pointed and muttered as I flew past. I tried to avoid them, scrambling up steps and under hedges to the shadowy lands behind their giant dens.

I sensed that the foxes were still behind me, edging along buildings, just out of sight.

I thought of Pirie and our games, the safety and comfort of his muzzle on my neck. My pace quickened.

My mind was a jumble. Why did those foxes come? What did they want?

I was scarcely aware of the world that whirred past my whiskers. The buildings were all a blur. I knew only one thing: that my family was gone, that our den was abandoned.

I had to find them.

* * *

A mangler howled and the ground thundered.

I leaped across its path without daring to look. In an instant I was panting on the far side of the deathway. I shied against a wall as other manglers careened past, glaring at me with white eyes.

Manglers were the greatest hazards of the Snarl—boxy, hulking beasts with spinning paws and arched backs. They stared ever forward with bright, unblinking eyes, prowling the endless coil of stone paths we called the deathway. Their bodies were strangely hollow, and the furless rode within them. Though the deathway might look empty and quiet one moment, this was just another furless trap. Manglers were deadly fast.

I remembered Greatma's warnings: "The death river claims more foxes than all other assassins."

But the deathway was everywhere, impossible to avoid. Its many claws etched paths through the Snarl where shimmering manglers hunted night and day.

I had to find the place where the deathway ended. But no matter how far I ran, it was always there . . . What if it went on forever? My legs quivered with exhaustion, refusing to be still. I struggled to catch my breath. When I blinked, I saw echoes of the burning fires of the Great Snarl, the floating brightglobes, the blazing eyes of manglers. It was a land of gray walls and hard dens, broken ground and thumping beats. My head spun and I clamped my eyes shut, waiting for the world to slow down around me.

At least I'd eluded the foxes. There was no hint of their scent on the evening air. But in doing so, I'd lost my way. I cowered as another mangler screeched past me on the death-way. I wasn't supposed to be here. Greatma's voice again, inside my head, wrestling against the din of the Great Snarl: "The death river is the furless's cruelest trick. Tread it rarely. Never trust it, no matter how calm it seems." She'd be furious if she found out how many times I'd crossed it tonight. My brush sagged guiltily. But of course, Greatma wasn't where she should be either, not at the den.

I remembered the sharp tang of cinders, the scarlet embers that smoked without warmth . . . the trail of blood. I knew instinctively that the vixen with the gray eye would return to our patch with her horrible skulk. I was better off far from that place, and so was my family. If only we were together.

It was neither day nor night in the land of the furless. No trace of the sun remained in the sky, but brightglobes hung on straight-backed trunks, lighting the paths of the furless when it grew dark. I could hear their whispering hisses and feel the faint vibration of their thrumming. Dark clouds eddied above them, sticky with the promise of rain.

Clusters of furless dens blocked the horizon. Gleaming

spy holes were cut in their dark frames, and I saw movement within: a furless prowling; the flicker of colorful screens. Turning slowly, gazing up, I noticed that the dens seemed to rise in one direction, creeping higher and higher into the sky. Perhaps up there it was possible to look over the Great Snarl—to get a better view.

To find my family.

I stole along the bank of the deathway, making my way to the higher climbs. The Great Snarl was a grimy maze of fences and dead ends, of mesh and wire as sharp as talons. The furless liked their walls.

Walls to keep them in.

Walls to keep others out.

The Great Snarl was full of them.

My legs were throbbing but I couldn't rest. I trod along the graystone. I could feel myself rising, constantly rising, and when I looked back I saw the path behind me roll downhill. I couldn't see far—a building blocked my view—but I was encouraged. When I reached the top of the Great Snarl, the world would be clearer. I'd know what to do.

At last the ground leveled out into something that resembled a wildway. I was comforted by the scent of earth and whimpered with relief as my aching paws sank onto the grass bank. This wildway was much larger than the one by our patch. The grass was strangely short, as if gnawed to stumps. It sprawled across a hill, with tall trees circled by colorful plants. There was a building in the middle surrounded by fences.

I turned to look out over the Snarl with a sigh. It was a twinkling constellation of brightglobes. The ugly gray dens of the furless had evaporated amid the glow. In the distance, I could see a huddle of towering buildings. They rose in strange shapes and sparkled like frost. One was pointed like fox ears. Another was round. But most were square, like furless dens, though even from this distance I could tell they were a great deal taller. Light shimmered from the buildings, enough to rival the sun. From this vantage point, it was almost beautiful.

I could not make sense of the crisscross of tiny gray lines beneath the brightglobes of the Snarl, which disguised the many tributaries of the deathway. I squinted my eyes and tried to pick out details.

Down there, a skulk of foxes was haunting the graystone with their ash-tipped fur.

Down there, was my family searching for me?

I lifted my muzzle to look for clouds. At last I saw the moon, a yellow ball in the dreary sky. My brush curled around my flank. The clouds were drifting, cloaking the moon in a hazy pelt. Its light paled against the brightglobes below.

I turned to the building, head cocked. It was different from others I'd seen. Instead of the usual walls of the Great

Snarl I saw circles within circles of fences. Not the wooden kind, like the one that separated our patch from the neighboring wildway. These fences reached into the sky and looked as hard as stone, each upright bar an evenly spaced black railing.

I padded toward the building, curiosity twitching at the base of my tail. A path cut between the grass, leading toward an archway over what looked like two great, closed doors. I avoided the archway and skirted around the bars for a few brush-lengths before slipping between them with ease.

It was as though I'd stumbled into an invisible mist. The air around me crackled with the scent of unfamiliar beasts: woody, fragrant, pungent, acrid . . .

I raised a forepaw and hesitated. There were creatures nearby, lots of them. They weren't foxes, they weren't furless . . . I smelled pelts, feathers, and leathery skin. Ahead of me, further bars were cast in darkness. I paused, struggling to disentangle the jumble of odors, growing woozy with the effort.

I started to turn back toward the deathway. I didn't like this place.

Then I heard a squawk and my belly growled excitedly. Something tasty lived here. My ears pricked and I stepped lightly on my paws. I could still sense other creatures. From the strong, fleshy stench, some must have been large—even larger than the furless. I guessed they were sleeping, as I couldn't detect movement. I had to be careful not to disturb them.

Beyond further bars, there were cages. A lower fence ran around the outside—nearly as tall as a furless. The bars of the low fence were widely spaced. I slid between them cautiously.

Why did the furless keep creatures in cages? What was this place for?

I took a step toward the closest den and spotted the outline of a great beast lying on its side. Its skin was thick as a tree's bark, and its face was wide and heavy with a pointed horn. It didn't even twitch as I passed, oblivious to my presence.

My stomach was churning, but a sense inside me urged caution. There was something very wrong with these strange beast dens, something *unnatural*. Again I wondered why the furless built this place of traps. Did they plan to kill the creatures and feast on their flesh? Why did they hoard so many?

I moved along the narrow bars to another den. I smelled dried grass and mud inside the cage—I couldn't work out what lived in there. There was a wooden structure where the creature must have slept. I sensed it was harmless—an eater of grasses, not flesh and bone.

By the third den, I paused to draw in gulps of air. My head was buzzing from all the odors. I closed my eyes, allowing the smells to fall into place. The creatures nearest to me had thick hides or pelts of fur. Deeper along the cages I was sure I smelled feathers. That's where I needed to go: to the birds.

To the one that squawked, announcing itself, inviting my approach.

I was heading the wrong way. As I opened my eyes and began to turn, I was struck by a pungent, musky odor. It was coming from the den in front of me. I couldn't see any movement. I crept closer.

The cage was empty now, but I could tell that something had recently lived there. Instinct hissed in my ears like an icy wind. Yet curiosity compelled me . . . I peered through the bars. There was a patch of grassy earth, some shrubs, and a small pond. I strained to see further. Nearer to the bars, a tree had been hacked to a stump. Parallel grooves ran along the bark.

Giant claw marks.

A shiver ran down my back. The grooves were many times deeper than anything a fox could do. A creature of great power had been in this den.

I caught a whiff of something tasty. My eyes seized on a bone not far from the bars. There was a hunk of meat hanging off it, with globs of white gristle. My belly rumbled excitedly. I stretched a forepaw through the bars. I couldn't quite reach the bone. Yipping in frustration, I tried again. My claws prodded the bone, which shifted a whisker closer.

I remembered how calmly Ma had eased some berries from a high branch, using one forepaw to draw the branch down and the other to hold it still. If I was patient, I could retrieve the bone. This close I could almost taste it. I imagined the fatty meat in my mouth, the juices running down my throat.

Another careful bat of the paw and it was almost close enough to snatch. The hunk of meat was pink and smelled delicious. The bone was long and white as teeth. There were dents across its surface. Something had gnashed at the bone with mighty jaws.

I squeezed my paw further between the bars. Halfway up my foreleg I could feel the pinch. But my belly's complaints were louder.

I'm hungry, it told me.

It's late, I've not eaten.

Gritting my teeth, I shoved my leg deeper and nudged the bone. I lowered my snout, opening my mouth to scoop it up. This low to the ground, the scent of the creature was powerful. Its musk stung at the base of my jaw. My body tensed. I didn't feel right about this . . . The scent was too strong, too fresh—

A roar exploded from the dark side of the den. A monstrous thing bounded toward me. I jerked at my paw and yelped in pain. My foreleg was trapped! I crumpled with terror as the monster threw himself against the bars, his massive jaws expanding with a furious howl. Other creatures stirred in nearby dens. The squawking started up again, and I cursed the bird that lured me to this horrifying place. I yanked and twisted but couldn't pull myself free.

The beast dropped on all fours. His eyes were yellow like the moon, edged in darkest black. His frame was that of a giant dog, but with his broad shoulders and wild eyes, he looked much more savage. Pointed ears framed his enormous head. His shaggy white fur was flecked with gray, falling about him like a knotted mane.

"Fox-ka!" he growled in a voice as deep and dark as the earth. "Conniving, crafty wretch!"

I was astonished to understand his words. He must have been a cub of Canista—a creature like me—though I could hardly imagine how we might be related. What was this monster, this giant dog with fire in his eyes?

He dropped his shaggy head. His black lips curled back, wet with spit. "You have the nerve to steal *my* food?" he snarled. Wrinkles coursed his muzzle. Beneath his black lips his gums were pink, and his fangs were as large as a fox's paw.

I opened my mouth but my tongue was dry, and the sound I made was barely a whimper. I was mesmerized by fear, by the frenzied rage in his yellow eyes. He glowered and I looked away, yearning for the comfort of my old life. Fa and Ma never warned me about monsters like this. If only they were here to help, to tell me what to do.

The creature pressed his muzzle near mine. "Speak!"

Although I didn't look up, I could still feel his eyes boring into me. I cowered, lost for words.

My silence seemed to enrage him. "You have disrespected me, Fox-ka, eater of broken meats! You are a thief without honor, and now you will pay!" My eyes darted up to see the soft pink folds of his tongue. It was hard to imagine that a thing so fragile could hide in such a ferocious creature.

I tugged at my leg but couldn't free myself.

I wasn't even sure why he was angry. Was it because of the bone? "I eat rats!" I cried as he rolled back on his haunches.

His face contorted with disgust. "Rats?" he rasped with a twitch of his ears. "A thing that eats rats has no right to exist!"

I had just enough time to see his fangs yawn wide. Beyond the pink of his tongue, there was darkness.

3

I flailed and bucked, desperate to free my trapped foreleg. The creature's great jaws gaped above me; I felt the dampness of his breath. My eyes rolled to the sky, where banks of gray were shifting. A cluster of stars pierced the clouds, brighter than the Great Snarl's yellow beams. They shimmered with flecks of fire. Canista's Lights! My Fa had spoken of them—of the stars that he'd seen as a cub.

A surge of warmth ran through me.

My panic ebbed.

I fixed my gaze on the lights. The world around them faded, and with it the mighty creature bearing down on me.

I was flesh without bone.

I was limber and lean.

With the lights prickling the back of my eyes, I gave a sharp tug and was free. I tumbled back on the safe side of the bars. The creature's fangs snapped whiskers away from me—a moment later and I'd have lost my paw. My eyes darted up the bars: even a beast of his size couldn't scale them.

His snout smacked against them with a clunk. "Fox-ka!" he howled. "Rat-munching coward!" He jammed his black nose between the bars, thumping them with a paw that was far too wide to reach through the gap.

I rose with a yelp, collapsing back onto the ground. My foreleg stung from the hard bite of the bars. It pulsed with pain when I put weight on it. I examined it for blood but found none. I rolled unsteadily onto my three good legs, folding the injured forepaw against my chest.

A piercing yellow eye stared between the bars. "Off to steal someone else's food? Or are you simply here to gawk at the trapped beasts, like the furless?"

My instincts told me to bolt but I fought against them, determined to return the beast's gaze. He could snarl all he wanted, but he couldn't escape the den.

I met his eyes.

My terror was waning, but my glance snagged on those yellow orbs. Whiskers of gold ran through them in complex patterns. Against their flinty outlines, they glowed with brooding power.

I swallowed hard. "I'm not a thief."

I thought of the bone with the hunk of meat. It was there, by his side in the den. I was so close . . . "I didn't know it was yours," I mumbled. "I thought no one wanted it." I stopped short of saying sorry.

His muzzle wrinkled. "So you're a *scavenger*."

I remembered something Greatma would say: "You do what you must to survive."

The beast's ears swiveled. "What of dignity and honor? Have you no shame, Fox-ka?"

I wasn't sure what he meant. What did he expect me to eat?

He waited for a response. When I didn't offer him one, he slid along the side of the bars, down to my level. "Can you come a little closer, Fox-ka? Will you not give this old wolf some sport?"

A jolt of alarm shot through me.

Wolf.

I'd heard that word before. Fa spoke of noble creatures, the greatest sons and daughters of Canista. But as I stared at the beast behind the bars, it was hard to imagine they were more than brutal killers.

I limped from his den toward the lower fence and the Great Snarl beyond them with its speckles of light, though I still watched the wolf from the corner of my eye. I knew he couldn't escape, but I wasn't prepared to turn my back on him.

"Where are you going, Fox-ka?" he rasped.

I paused, brush swishing. For the first time I noticed

that his pelt was knotted. I looked more closely. There were furrows in the fur at his muzzle where it had rubbed away, revealing charcoal skin. He must have been shoving it repeatedly between the bars, over and over for untold days. His claws were split and dirty and his feathery tail was limp. I squinted through the bars, exploring the dark den. Fa told me that wolves prowled the Snowlands in packs, beyond the Raging River: deadly armies, distant kingdoms.

This wolf was alone.

I looked to the sky, but Canista's Lights were hidden once more beyond the swirling clouds. "To find my family." Saying this out loud hurt like a claw hooked in my chest. I stifled a whimper.

The wolf watched in silence as I started to move away again.

When he spoke, his voice was low. "Fox-ka is solitary. What can you know of loyalty to something greater than yourself? Family means nothing to you." It was a statement, not a question.

Anger crackled through my fur. He could sneer all he wanted about what I ate—but he'd better leave my family out of it. "You're wrong," I yelped, swinging around to meet his eye. "You don't know anything, *Wolf*! Ma, Fa, and Greatma were chased away. My brother, Pirie, too. They're somewhere out in the Snarl, and I'm going to find them!"

The beast's ears flicked back—he hadn't expected that. Lip crinkling, he glared at me, slaughter in his eyes. But this time the tall bars were on my side.

I slipped through the next set of bars. When I reached the fence that bordered the wildway, I glanced back at the beast dens—back at the wolf. He was sprawled on his belly, his huge head resting on his forepaws. From this distance I couldn't see his eyes, but I knew he was still watching. I wondered where he was from and how he came to be here, so far from his own kind.

His words echoed in my mind. *Are you simply here to gawk at the trapped beasts, like the furless?*

My brush curled around my flank. Is that what this place was? A source of entertainment for the furless?

Both anger and fear had faded. Now I felt only pity for the wolf. He may not have chased rats, or eaten the food that the furless left behind. He may have longer fangs and sharper claws than me. He may have been larger and fiercer than any fox, any dog. But for all that, he was a prisoner, and I was free.

My foreleg didn't hurt much if I kept my weight off it, but it was slowing me down. I limped along the winding deathway, cutting a new path through the Great Snarl. I had to stop regularly to rest.

I sniffed the air and smelled the foul breath of the

manglers. They rumbled along: stretched ones, fat ones, red ones, black ones, glowering with eyes of fire. *The death river.* That's what Greatma called it. Real rivers were full of water, like ponds without beginning or end—I knew that from Fa, who had seen them in the Wildlands. But I had learned something about the Great Snarl without my family's help. The beasts of the deathway never scaled its borders, as though they were fish that lacked the cunning to climb out of the water. The furless seemed to understand this, wandering carefree on its raised banks. I spotted some climbing inside manglers, or blinking from within, looking quite untroubled. I ran my claws through my tangled whiskers, wondering why the manglers kept their distance, despite their snarls. I decided they were fearsome but foolish.

Watch! Wait! Listen!

By keeping to the banks of the deathway I had outwitted the manglers. Greatma would be proud of me. I longed to tell her about my discovery.

I longed to bury my head against her mottled shoulder.

A furless couple strolled in step, their forelegs intertwined. I shrank into the shadows. They purred and trilled, ignorant of my presence. Even the growl of a passing mangler did not distract them from one another. I watched them meander over the bank, cross the deathway, and disappear from view. I had expected to stand out in this graystone land, but most furless didn't even notice me. I remembered Ma telling me about their poor sense of smell, but it was more than that—it was as though I was invisible.

I slunk along the wall and hopped down several steps. Against the bank of the deathway, one of the manglers was sleeping. I peeled back my lips and yawned. My head felt heavy, clogged with earth and fur. I found myself envying the restful mangler. I took a tentative step toward it, but it was frozen and silent as a tree. I didn't fear it now. It was a lifeless thing. Its eyes neither stared nor blazed; they were wide but dark. I crawled beneath its belly and buried my head in my paws.

Sleep did not come.

With a weary sigh, I crept out from under the mangler and sniffed the air.

I caught the whiff of a young fox and spun around, Pirie's name on my breath. A moment later, the scent was gone.

I was so tired I no longer trusted my senses. The night was playing tricks on me. My stomach rumbled and I did my best to ignore it, slipping into a wildway. The grass was soft and low. If I could find a place to rest my head a while, I'd feel better. Then I'd search again, before the bustle of the day, when furless teemed onto the deathway and I'd be forced to retreat. To watch and wait.

I wound through the grass and breathed in the scent of the soil.

My ears pricked up. Once, when I was very young, with eyes scarcely open and ears still floppy, I'd heard a beautiful song in the air. The voice had spun in cheerful loops, brilliant like ice as a cold dawn broke. I was sure that singer was as large as a fox to command such a powerful tune. I had searched our patch, peered through grasses and branches, but I could not discover the master of the voice.

Now the same, sweet melody rose on the breeze. In the dark, against the hush of nearby manglers, it took on a haunting note. I looked about but saw nothing.

A moth fluttered blindly before my nose, settling onto a fallen leaf. With a pounce, I trapped it beneath my paws. I crunched the stiff wings with satisfaction. As I swallowed down the last of the moth, I took another sniff of the night air. A fox! This time I was sure of it, though it wasn't the same one I'd smelled earlier. And I knew immediately that it wasn't Greatma, Ma, or Fa. It wasn't a foxling either: I sensed this fox was old, perhaps unwell. There was something musty in her odor. Still, my heart gave a little skip. After the manglers, the furless, and the wolf, I was desperate to meet my own kind.

The beautiful song faded as she came into view, stepping out from behind a tree. She was old, like Greatma, and a surge of relief ran though me. Like Greatma, she'd be wise; she would understand, and would help me find my family. Her body was wiry, the fur patchy about her shoulders. I started bounding toward her with a trill, raising my nose to touch hers, but she shied away. Her hackles rose, a growl in her throat. Her face was angled to one side, her jaws parted in a sneer, and her tail shot out behind her.

I stopped dead.

"What are you doing here?" The old fox trod closer, her paws stumbling awkwardly over the grass. There was something wrong in the way she moved, a tightness through her hips. I saw grit at the corner of her eyes—one of them was only half-open.

"Are you sick?" I asked.

The old vixen squinted at me. "How is it your business?"

Nearby, a mangler screeched and a furless yowled a tuneless song.

"I just . . ." My words dried on my tongue. I could hardly contain my disappointment. I thought she'd be friendly.

The old fox stared, her wide ears splayed. "Well, what do you want?"

I started to take a step toward her but thought better of it. "My name is Isla and I'm looking for my family. My Ma and Fa, and my brother, Pirie."

This seemed to anger her. "Pirie?" she snarled. "I already told you that I don't know him. Get out of here!"

I stayed where I was, but my body was braced to run. The caged wolf had seethed with force, but I saw something more unsettling in the old fox's eyes. Beyond the ruins of age, there was spite.

What had Ma told me? "Never prey on a cat—a cat will fight."

"But they're small! They're weaker than foxes," I'd pointed out.

Ma had thrown me a stern look. "It isn't about a creature's strength, their age, or their size. If you see fight in their eyes, leave them alone. A fox's hunt is not a cruel or violent one. Angry claws draw blood."

I recalled this exchange with a wrinkle of unease. I wasn't safe with this old fox. I could probably outrun her—even with my injured foreleg—but if she caught me, she'd fight viciously.

Angry claws draw blood.

I tried not to show my fear when I replied. "You haven't told me anything yet. And I won't go, not till you do."

She looked at me in astonishment, champing at her fangs. A sharp scent caught my nose. I remembered the time I'd found a bowl of white water in the yard by the furless den. As I'd gone to taste it Ma had called me away.

"It's milk," she had told me, "but it is no longer good." There were blobs in the liquid like globules of fat. A sniff had confirmed that Ma was right. The scent had set my whiskers crinkling, and a lump of revulsion had risen in my throat.

The same smell clung to the old vixen—the smell of milk gone sour. "Leave me alone, cub."

The fur itched along my back. One of my hind legs trembled, and I pressed the paw hard against the earth. "Not until I've found them."

"There's no one here. This is *my* patch. Everything you see is *mine*. They're always trying to thieve it, to take my food. How many times do I need to tell you? Go away!"

My ears flicked back. It was the second time that night I'd been accused of stealing. "I don't want your food! I want Pirie and my family. My brother has an unusual coat, with patches of silver and gold."

The old fox scowled at me. Her brush fell limp, no longer springing out behind her. Her tongue lapped absently toward her squinting eye but failed to reach it. She muttered, her voice husky. "You come. You ask for Pirie. You go. You come. When will you leave me alone?"

I began to suspect that age and ill health had clawed channels of confusion in the old fox's mind. I sipped the vapors of the night: grass, earth, the acid pall of the deathway, the diseased breath of its stalking manglers. There was no scent of Pirie on the air, nothing to link Ma, Fa, or Greatma to this place.

I backed away a few paces. The old fox growled, perhaps sensing victory. Her bones seemed to swell and her tufty back arched.

I slipped onto the bank of the deathway. The vixen did not give chase. Her voice was triumphant as she yelped after me: "Forget your family, if you have any sense. A fox's burden is heavy, why carry more weight?"

My ears twitched, rotated.

It didn't matter what she thought.

I turned the corner onto a quiet stretch of the deathway. Aching with loneliness, I crawled under a bush to get some rest. As I peered beneath the branches, I could barely make out the fenced-in structure over the Snarl with its lofty bars and shaded dens. I couldn't see inside the cages. I could only remember the smell of beasts and the fearsome wolf with the moon in his eyes.

There was a tap on my nose, another on my ear, the cool sting of water.

I blinked, craning my head beneath the bush, sleep addled and afraid. Greatma was right: with the first hint of dawn, the rain had come.

The air was heavy—a downpour was on its way. I shrugged free of the bush and started to search for a better place to hide, a shelter where I could sleep through the day. A *click-click-click* sounded behind me and I turned sharply. My hackles rose, my ears swiveled around, but there was no one there. The hairs on my neck were pointy spikes.

Along a wall, near a huddle of thorns, I found a small wooden den with the broken remains of a tree piled inside. I scrambled through a gap in the den and climbed over the wood, which quivered beneath my paws. I licked my foreleg. The pain was almost gone, but even when I shifted I couldn't get comfortable. I had never slept without my brother by my side. I wrapped my brush around my body, pretending it was Pirie. I closed my eyes and tried to imagine the warmth of the den. Instead, I remembered it as I'd last seen it, bitter with tendrils of smoke.

Another image came to me: a giant furless with the wings of a bird. How had it entered my thoughts? What did it mean?

I ached with exhaustion.

I tried not to think of the mad old fox, but her words played on my mind: *You come. You ask for Pirie. You go. You come.*

The sun was rising. Whiskers of light glanced through the bars of the den.

Already the Great Snarl was droning and clanking as I drifted to sleep.

And another sound, a *click-click-click*. Like long, ragged claws on hard stone.

Click-click-click.

4

A mouse! It shot along a row of furless dens, pausing on the bank of the deathway to inspect its long tail. I watched from the shadow cast by a sleeping mangler. A day had passed, and the sun's grimy light was already sinking to dusk. My belly rumbled with hunger—I had only eaten a moth since my family disappeared, and that was a night ago. Mice were difficult, I knew: fast, wily, shrewder than moths. Tastier too, more meat on them.

Pirie was a better hunter than I was. He had tried to teach me on a chill dawn while the furless slept.

"Hold your breath, Isla. Tense your body. If you move your brush, it won't work."

My breath had snared in my throat. It was an unbearable feeling. Panic had swelled inside me, replacing the rise and fall of my chest.

"Stay calm. Nothing will to happen to you. Now drop your body low to the—Isla! You breathed!"

I couldn't help it. "It isn't natural."

His brush had tapped the grass. We were standing in our patch, not far from our den. Ma, Fa, and Greatma were stalking the wildway. "You're too impatient. All foxes do it. It's just part of hunting."

"You can keep your tricks. I don't need them." That wasn't true. While I was smaller and more adept at working my way through narrow gaps, I wasn't much good at catching prey. "It's only because you're bigger than me. You can run faster."

Pirie had cocked his head to one side. "To hunt you need patience more than speed. Patience. Silence. Focus. Like a cat."

"Cats are nasty."

"They're good hunters."

I snorted, not convinced. "They can't hunt like foxes, can't make themselves invisible or imitate birdcalls."

"They're light as clover on their paws. They don't need illusions."

I had thought of the overfed ginger tom who lived near our den, always glaring at us and flicking his tail. "Shifty. Cunning. Endlessly grooming. Nipping and licking and preening all day. What do they care what their fur smells like? It hardly smells at all. No wonder they can sneak up on rats. Fur without smell—now *that* isn't natural."

"Isla! You're impossible! Stop wasting time and concentrate." But instead I had sprung on him and nipped his ear with a playful growl in my throat. We had rolled in the grass, kicking up a shower of dewdrops.

I blinked away the memory. The mouse was still by the furless dens, perching on its hind paws. The deathway was quiet. A couple of manglers lay asleep by the bank, but none came charging with their white eyes blazing.

I thought about creeping up on the mouse.

It was too far away to chase.

If it saw me, detected me, it would run.

I sucked in my breath and tensed my body. I tried to remember how to hold myself—was my tail supposed to shoot straight out behind me? Did it help if my ears were pricked? If only I had paid more attention when Pirie had tried to explain . . .

Forcing myself not to blink, I focused on the mouse. It hadn't spotted me watching from the shadows. Its whiskers fluttered tirelessly as its beady eyes roved over the graystone.

Very slowly, I raised a forepaw. I held it suspended for several beats, waiting for the mouse to look at me. Instead it swiveled its head the other way, toward the wall. I could hardly believe my luck. I risked a step in its direction. Another step. My breath was pulsing at my throat, but I swallowed it down as I crept closer to the mouse. Still it made no move to run. A shiver of excitement ran through me. Could it see me? Was I invisible?

My breath clawed hotly at my jaw, suddenly unbearable. I bit, I snapped—too far, not yet!

My breath escaped in an explosion. I gasped it back but it was too late—the mouse was gawking at me with startled eyes. It sprang into the air like a flea. I pounced, but already it had shinnied up a wall and out of my reach.

My brush drooped.

Pirie would have caught it.

The last light of dusk had settled beyond the skyline. The mouse was gone, and my belly ached with hunger. I was reduced to treading grass banks for earthworms. I scraped against the soil with my front paws, buried my nose between rocks, and yanked out whatever I found. I chomped enough worms to stave off hunger and crunched my way through several beetles. I washed away the bitter aftertaste by drinking from puddles.

I strolled to a quiet bank of the deathway where a lone furless peered inside a bin. These waterless hollows were dotted around the land of the furless, and there was sometimes a meal to be found in them. Rifling through one, Fa had once discovered an entire bird. It was naked of feathers, like a large, headless pigeon. We buried it in our cache and fed from it for days.

I heard the shuffle of paws on hard ground and swung around, my fur puffing instinctively. A small, ugly dog stood at the edge of the deathway. His brown fur was wiry, and a rope hung loosely around his neck. He glanced at me and I arched my back. He was still far away. He wouldn't be able to catch me—just let him try to get any nearer.

The mongrel flicked his tail and yawned. He padded away into the night.

A cackle rose from the deathway, and I turned back to look. A skulk of four furless were striding toward me. One pointed and yipped in surprise, batting the foreleg of her friend. I made as though to run, but the furless beckoned. I could tell they were young by their smooth skin and swift movements. One unwrapped a hunk of brown food. Even from a distance I could smell something sweet, and a hidden delight, a chunk of meat. The furless extended his hand, holding out the food. The aroma grew stronger, and I ran my tongue over my lips. It smelled better than beetles and worms. My belly churned with hunger.

I took a step closer.

The furless with the food was yipping gently.

He crept toward me, leading with the hand that clutched the food. The other furless watched him, exchanging low barks.

I tried to think what Ma and Pa would say if they saw me taking food from a furless in the deathway. I *knew* what they'd say.

Stay away! The furless can't be trusted.

But Ma and Pa weren't here.

I stepped closer, so close that the food was almost in reach.

Suddenly the furless whipped his paw away, and the others burst into high-pitched cackles. One of them grabbed a rock and flung it at me. It struck the stone ground by my hind paw, and I sprang back in confusion. My heart jerked against my chest. The young furless shrieked as I bolted down the deathway. When I reached the corner, I stole a quick look back. They were waving their forepaws, leaning against each other.

It was a game to them . . .

I almost crashed into an old male furless who was stumbling along the bank of the deathway. A sharp smell rose off him. I crossed the deathway, climbing beneath a sleeping mangler to watch him. There was a heaviness in his movements. His robes hung loosely on his body, which reeked of neglect.

There was something desperate about this creature.

He propped himself up against a wall. I waited to see if another furless would appear to bring him food. I could hear the young furless skulk cackling beyond the bend in the deathway, their voices drifting as they moved away.

Nobody came.

The old furless was shuffling toward the entrance of a huge den. Up a couple of shadowy steps, a pair of brown eyes watched him. The hairs rose along my back. The furless hadn't noticed, hardly looking as he lurched toward the doorway. A mangler rumbled around the corner.

I thought I saw a stocky creature—perhaps a fox—spring down the steps from the shady entrance to the building. I spotted a thick gray coat—it could have been a fluffy cat. Its eyes flashed green as it caught my gaze before the mangler rushed to obscure my view. I blinked, craning my head. When the mangler had passed, the creature was gone.

The furless dropped heavily onto the steps at the entrance to the den. He leaned against the wall, rocking himself and mumbling. Soon he fell asleep. I watched him for a moment, flexing my whiskers. I could not understand the Great Snarl. Some furless lived in dens with their families while others curled alone at their entrances.

It was always better to be close to family.

I thought of Ma and Fa. Where would they go in this

vast land of graystone? They knew it so well. I remembered Fa's stories of his youthful days roving. Unlike Ma and Greatma, he came from the Wildlands, far away. He told me and Pirie it was different there: the days were longer; the nights were darker. Canista's Lights twinkled in the sky, the way they never did in the "Graylands"—that's what foxes from the Wildlands called the Great Snarl. Fa missed the lights most of all.

He'd left the Wildlands because there were no young females nearby and he was keen to start a family of his own. He had heard that the Great Snarl was a place of plenty, where each fox could find a mate, and rats big as cats were there for the taking. One night he dreamed he met a beautiful vixen with a ginger coat, the urban fox who was to be the future ma of his cubs. He bid farewell to his sisters and his parents, walking without knowing where he'd end up.

"You left your home because of a dream?" I'd asked in amazement.

"You know what they say." Fa had cocked his head. "Dreams are the beginning."

He had walked a long time before the swathes of green vanished and the contours of the Great Snarl cut patterns in the skyline.

It was there he'd met Ma, the ginger-furred vixen, the very same fox he had seen in his dream. They'd started their lives together, with Greatma to help raise the cubs when they came along. And they came along early—me and Pirie, impatient even then. We couldn't wait to be born. Cubs usually arrived when it was warmer, and day and night were of equal length—Greatma had told us that.

"But the sky?" Pirie had asked Fa. "Is it really different here?"

Fa had looked to the twisting pelt of gray overhead. "Very different," he'd murmured. "We cannot see Canista's Lights at all."

I gave Fa a nudge. "Don't you miss them?"

His eyes had taken on a distant look. "They are beautiful. I long to see them one more time . . ." He'd shaken out his fur and caught my eye. "But I would give all the lights in the sky for what I have here in the Great Snarl—for my life with your ma, your greatma, and the two of you."

"What about those tasty rabbits?" Pirie's tongue had lolled from his mouth.

Fa had cocked his head. "Rabbits?" He'd trilled like a cub. "I would give every rabbit of the Wildlands for a couple of our delicious rats."

The furless was snoring at the entrance to the den. Something was stalking along the stone ground, sniffing quite boldly at his hind paw where the pelt had come loose, revealing pink skin.

A rat.

A delicious rat from the Great Snarl!

It was like a message from Fa. I started slinking behind the rat, easing my paws down silently, one in front of the other. It hadn't noticed me yet. It was tasting the skin of the furless's paw with its long, pointy tongue. Losing interest, it scuttled along the deathway, not even keeping to the wall as the mouse had. There was something fearless, almost challenging, in the rat's bumbling movements.

I would make myself invisible. I would hold my breath—I would be patient.

But I'd missed my chance. Although it didn't turn its head, by some fiendish instinct the rat must have guessed I was there. Without warning it burst into a run. It whizzed along the stone ground with a speed that seemed impossible for such a loping stride. I found I was running too. My mouth filled with spit and my belly growled—I would catch this rat if it was the last thing I did!

It scurried over the deathway and turned a corner, but I was close behind it, my eyes locked on its knotty tail. It made for the side of a furless den. I knew that rats, like mice, could shinny up rock. In a moment the rat would be up the den and out of my reach. I thought of the bird that crowed in our wildway. Tossing back my head, I threw my voice into the night.

"Caw! Caw!"

The birdcall boomed above the furless den. The rat leaped back, startled, and changed direction. My trick had worked! The chase was still on.

But the rat was determined. It lurched across another length of the deathway toward a wooden fence. Flanking both sides of the fence was a high, redstone wall. I could guess the rat's plan—it would scurry to freedom, leaving me stuck on the wrong side of the fence. My chest swelled with determination: never underestimate a fox!

Instead of running for the fence, I changed direction, making for a bin by a wall at the side of the deathway. A mangler swerved around the corner, and my heart lurched. I cleared the deathway just as it whizzed by—its hard, shiny shell almost clipped me. With a gasp I was safe on the far bank. My thumping chest and hunger were making me reckless. I jumped for the bin at the side of the wall, leaping so high that I almost flew straight over it. A quick scramble and I found my balance, teetering on the edge of the bin. I risked a glimpse down at the rat. It was scrambling beneath the wooden fence, just as I had guessed it would.

This wasn't over yet.

From the trough, I sprang onto the redstone wall. There wasn't much to see on the far side of the wall—just a large, abandoned yard with a graystone floor. And there was the rat. It thought it was safe, I could tell. It sat a short distance from the wooden fence, staring over its shoulder. It knew that a fox couldn't follow it beneath the fence. It didn't know that I was hovering above it, waiting for the moment to pounce.

My forepaw slipped on the wall—it was the one I had caught between the bars at the wolf's den. I grappled for a foothold and the rat's head shot up. It saw me, gave a startled squeak, and bolted across the graystone.

Isla, you idiot! I thought with frustration. I sprang off the high wall, thumping down onto the ground. The rat was already out of reach. If I'd only kept quiet a moment longer. If only I had Pirie's patience.

I took a deep breath. The chase was over—and after so much effort. How did Ma and Fa do it? I shook off my fur and fought to regain my breath. With a sigh, I sank onto the ground, my belly cool against the stone. The rat was looking back at me, a taunting glint in its eyes. It didn't see the dark figure stepping out from the far wall. A huge dog emerged from the shadows. Her muscles flexed beneath her shimmering black pelt. She slammed a great paw across the rat's back. Her square jaws clamped over its body and she snapped its neck with a single shake of her head. Tossing the rat on the floor beside her, she locked her eyes on mine.

"Fox!" she snarled. "Bad, bad fox! How dare you enter my territory?" She started toward me with thumping steps, her head dropped to her shoulders. I sprang to my paws, glancing up at the wall. There was no bin on this side, and it was too high to reach without something to climb on.

I was giddy with fear. "I didn't know anyone was here."

There was a metal chain around the black dog's neck. It jangled as she moved. "I guard this place for the furless," she spat. "They expect me to keep it free of intruders. I take my duties seriously." She came to a halt a few brush-lengths away from me. Her lips peeled back, flashing sharp white teeth. "*You* are an intruder."

Wildly, my eyes shot over the yard, desperate for a way out. Along the far wall, I spotted a gap where the redstone had crumbled. Sheets of wood were stacked against it, but these left a narrow passage at ground level. Was it big enough for me to escape? Would I make it there before she reached me? The black dog's muscles rippled at her flanks. I remembered how quickly she'd dispensed with the rat, and my mouth went dry with terror.

I risked a second glance at the wall. To my alarm, the wood sheets shifted. I was met by a pair of dark eyes. A wiry face poked out from behind the wood. It was the dog I had seen on the deathway that evening—the small, ugly dog with a rope around his neck. He snarled as he shoved his way through the gap in the wall, knocking down the wood sheets. They clattered to the ground, but he ignored them, his eyes fixed on me. His hackles rose and he ran his tongue over his muzzle. I took in his claws and his pointy teeth. But his look was the most threatening thing about him: there was something knowing in those eyes. Something that couldn't be trusted.

I spun around, my paws scrambling beneath me. The black dog had taken a step forward. Her jaw quivered with rage and her fangs frothed with spit. I froze, my chest seizing with panic. I knew this time there was no way out—knew what dogs did when they caught our kind. They'd tear me to strips just to teach me a lesson. All trace of me would be lost to the night, all memory of my family forgotten forever.

Mad fox.

Bad fox.

Just another dead fox.

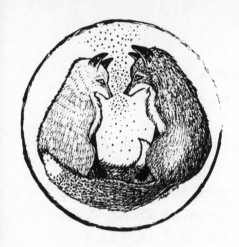

5

My eyes darted to the wiry mongrel and back to the dog with the glossy black coat. An icy chill cut through me. My limbs were frozen to the ground. I couldn't even place one paw in front of the other, and where would I go? The dogs were on either side of me. There was nowhere to run.

The black dog seemed more enraged than ever. "How *dare* you enter my territory!" she barked. Her dark eyes bulged and I saw the whites. The muscles bunched at her broad shoulders as she prepared to attack.

"Watch me!" It was the wiry dog. He jogged alongside the wall with a superior air that hardly fit his small, ugly body. A rich smell fanned across the yard and my whiskers pulsed—it was not the smell of a dirty dog. Was someone else here? My gaze skittered across the yard, but there was no one around. Just the two dogs—and me between them.

"I'll rip you to shreds!" the black dog barked. Her voice was so loud that it scraped my ears. But when I looked at her I realized her attention had shifted. Her furious eyes tracked the wiry mongrel as he strutted further into the yard. I couldn't understand what I had missed. Then it dawned on me: they weren't part of a pack—they were enemies.

The wiry dog yawned, as if all this bored him. Why was he here? Was he crazy?

The black dog roared with anger, great globs of white foam frothing at her jaws. Her lips curled back above her gums, revealing a double row of ragged teeth. "No one enters here and lives!" Her barrel chest puffed up with fury. "I killed a cat the other night."

"A cat? Really?" The mongrel couldn't have sounded less interested as he nibbled the end of his forepaw. He wasn't even *looking* at her.

The black dog growled in frustration. She sprang back on her hindquarters and charged at him—but the small dog was faster. He dodged, darting along the redstone wall. The black dog ran with so much force that she didn't have time to stop. She collided against the wall with a howl of pain. As she drew herself back, I saw her nose was bleeding. She shook her head, blood and spit splattering onto the graystone.

Turning awkwardly on her thickset limbs, her eyes sought out the little dog. She didn't seem to notice me at all—as though I'd become invisible.

The small dog was standing against the far wall. He looked like he was waiting for the black dog to come for him. He seemed strangely calm—even relaxed. If I hadn't known better, I'd have thought his tail was wagging.

Sure enough, the black dog charged toward him with her huge head dropped low. Again, the small dog leaped out of the way, pounding across the yard and goading her to follow him. As the black dog growled, her body shaking with fury, the mongrel threw a glance in my direction. Those knowing eyes. Flecked with bronze, like the light of dusk. A warm tremor ran through me. The icy feeling began to pass and blood rushed to my paws.

The black dog was snorting through her snout, snarling and frothing as she squared up to the mongrel. As she ran at him I spun around and made for the gap where the wall had crumbled away. A volley of barks broke out behind me. The black dog was raging, incoherent, her voice cracking with hate. She must have missed him again. She didn't seem to notice that I had left her territory, or she no longer cared. Her fight was with the mongrel now.

I could hardly believe my luck. I'd thought I was dead.

What was the small dog thinking? Didn't he realize she'd

break his neck? He must have no wit in his head. But those knowing eyes . . . He didn't seem stupid.

Moving quickly—but remembering to check the death-way for manglers—I cleared as much distance as possible. I found a passage into the grassy patches behind the dens of the furless and crept through these, foraging for worms. The yard with the dogs was far away now. My breathing eased.

No more dumb risks, Isla.

Watch! Wait! Listen!

I had to eat enough so that I had strength to go on. Worms were hard to find. I sighed as I spotted another beetle. I slammed my forepaws on its shell, but as I thought of the bitter aftertaste, I couldn't bring myself to eat it. Maybe I wasn't that hungry after all.

I remembered something that Greatma had said: "Since the dawn of time, our kind has been hunted: tortured, attacked, and turned into pelts to warm the necks of the furless. They have shot us for fun and chased us as a game— they do not even eat those they kill. By the death river or their casual cruelty; by gas, or dogs, or simple starvation. The land of the furless is full of deaths and each one whispers a fox's name."

Her solemn words had frightened me. "But we're still here," I'd pointed out.

She had cocked her head. "There are many ways for a fox to die—but only one way for her to live."

"What's that?" I'd asked, eyes wide, ears pricked.

"We choose to survive, as that is our legacy. We choose to live, and we never give up."

Her words had disappointed me. Was that the answer I'd been waiting for? That we live because we want to? That hardly made any sense. But as I watched the beetle trapped between my paws, I thought I knew what Greatma meant.

I choose to survive. I will never give up.

This thought made it easier to swallow the beetle—even the bitter shell.

I must have eaten my own weight in beetles. I curled up next to the trunk of a tree, drawing my brush around my body. At least I wasn't hungry anymore, though I'd have done anything for a single mouthful of rat. I hoped that wherever my family was, they had eaten well. I tried to imagine the smell of Ma's fur or the tickle of Fa's whiskers when he licked my nose. I felt these memories fading, and my ears pricked in alarm. But when I thought of Pirie, the image remained bright. I could picture every detail of his amber eyes, his black-tipped ears, and his colorful coat.

Soothed, I tucked my head beneath my forepaws and allowed my mind to drift. I remembered the den as it used to be, before the strange foxes had appeared with the scent of cinder. So warm and safe . . . Pirie and I were playing outside. Greatma was standing at the edge of the den, keeping a watchful eye on us while Ma and Fa hunted for food.

"Got you!" I snickered in a shrill explosion, catching Pirie's tail with my paws.

He jumped free, hopping on the grass and collapsing in a heap with his tongue lolling out of his mouth. I dropped at his side. He prodded me with his muzzle. "Little fox," he murmured.

The image faded and the world grew darker.

I felt myself being pulled away, a sharp voice snapping at my ear. I was jostled along a graystone path, flanked by hostile foxes as I stumbled over the deathway. I was moving with difficulty, my flank throbbing with pain. Up ahead there was a row of tall furless dens. In front of them was a huge stone yard with a lone furless standing at the center. Her skin was cool gray, her eyes stared blindly, and great wings unfolded from her back. I gazed at her in fear and wonder.

A twig cracked.

My head snapped up.

I was alert in an instant, casting my eyes into the darkness. I could make out the shrubs that ran along the fence. Maybe it had just been a mouse or a bird, nothing to worry about. I waited. The only movement was the gentle shudder of leaves in the wind. I began to relax, letting my gaze trail over the yard one last time. Then I noticed something shiny, a pair of dark eyes. My heart leaped and my whiskers bristled.

A creature was crouching by the shrubs, watching me. It seemed surprised that I'd spotted it—it too looked ready to flee.

I let out a small growl. "Who's there?"

The creature broke its cover, making toward the furless den. It was the wiry-furred dog.

I gasped in surprise. "You followed me!"

He didn't answer. With an impressive leap he sprang over the fence into the neighboring patch.

The dog's retreat gave me confidence. Before I knew what I was doing I was running at the fence. I didn't clear it as easily as he had—there was some flailing of paws as I hooked myself over, drawing up a back leg and launching myself at the grass on the other side. I landed clumsily. The wiry dog was trotting along the edge of a furless den. He reached a gate with widely spaced railings and shoved his head through. I saw him struggle to ease his body between the railings, but in a moment he'd managed it, disappearing onto the deathway.

I quickened behind him.

He was faster than me, but the gate had slowed him down. It was easy for me to slip between the railings. As I reached the deathway I saw him cross, glancing back with intense eyes.

I shouted after him. "What do you want?"

He turned away from me and started to run. My ears flicked back—what was he doing? Why had he been spying on me? I checked the deathway, but no manglers were passing. I dashed through it, chasing the dog as he bounded ahead. Soon he reached a point where two paths of the deathway crossed. He paused beneath a brightglobe, swiveling around. He seemed surprised to find me behind him. Up ahead I saw the top of giant buildings reaching over the furless dens. They loomed in strange shapes— pointed, round, angular . . . They were the buildings I had seen from my vantage point over the Great Snarl, before I'd encountered the wolf. Up close they sparkled like light on water.

"Stay away," snarled the dog, baring his teeth.

My attention snapped back to him. Anxiety clawed at my belly. He didn't *look* right. I frowned, gazing at his wiry fur. What was it? Then it struck me: although he stood beneath a brightglobe, the dog cast no shadow.

He must have seen something in my face that troubled him. He started running again. I followed him as fast as I could, my legs pumping, straining to keep up. We crossed the deathway where it swerved and grew larger. Tall buildings flanked us on both sides, their numerous spy holes humming with light. Their shells shone silver and their edges looked as sharp as claws.

A mangler thundered down the deathway. Its reflection glided across the surface of the nearest building before it sped out of view. But as the dog sprinted in front of me, a flash of red fur was mirrored in the shimmering building.

It wasn't the dog's reflection.

I stumbled, unsteady on my paws.

I'd glimpsed a fox!

As I gaped, jaw drooping, the dog ran clear of the building and reached a dead end. He skidded to a halt before a high stone wall and turned to look at me, his eyes unreadable.

I caught up with him, stopping a few brush-lengths away. He wasn't much bigger than me but he looked a lot stronger, with sharp yellow fangs and sturdy limbs. I knew from Greatma that small dogs could be more dangerous than larger ones. Some were trained by the furless to dig foxes from their dens and kill newborn cubs in their sleep.

I gritted my teeth and held my ground. "Who are you?" I panted. My legs started trembling. "*What* are you?"

The dog glanced across my shoulder at the shiny building. He seemed to understand what was disturbing me. The wind rose over the quiet deathway, tickling my whiskers. I could smell something on the air—a sweet, musky odor, the same scent I'd caught in the black dog's yard.

The mongrel ran his tongue over his muzzle. He spoke at last in a low voice. "My name is Siffrin. I am not what I seem . . . I am a messenger of Jana, one of the Elder Foxes from the Wildlands."

I blinked at him. "You . . . you're a messenger for a fox?" It didn't make any sense. "But you're a dog!"

"Like I said, I am not what I seem. I am in wa'akkir. I have assumed a disguise. It is safer."

"Safer for who?" I asked, anxiety creeping along my back. What could he mean?

The dog threw a quick look around. The deathway was quiet. "Keep your voice down," he snarled. "Safer for me . . . For the Elders. For you." He gave me a hard look. "Have you never heard of the Elders?"

The Elders.

My ears flicked back.

Now that he mentioned it, the term seemed faintly familiar, but I couldn't think why. "How long have you been following me?"

"I tracked you as you returned to your den and that skulk of foxes appeared." He dropped his gaze. "You didn't notice me before, though, did you? I haven't always looked the same."

"I saw you this evening," I growled defensively.

The dog flicked his tail. "For days I've watched you feasting on worms and crunching through beetles that dwell in dung mounds. I scarcely know how you survived. You leaped into the deathway without looking, practically let the furless stroke you like a pet. And tonight I was forced to save you from that guard dog. What on earth made a feeble foxlet think to go into that yard? Don't you sniff places out before you enter them?"

"I was chasing a rat," I mumbled, shame crackling through my fur in spite of myself. "You challenged that dog on purpose, so I could get away?"

His muzzle wrinkled with disapproval. "I did what I had to."

I remembered something—the sound of claws on graystone.

"I heard pawsteps that first night. It was you, following me!"

The dog snorted, an ugly sound. "You're deluded. You couldn't have heard me. I don't make any noise when I'm tracking someone—*not a whisper.*"

My head was whirring. I remembered the creature with the thick gray coat who had stared at me on my first night alone before disappearing behind a mangler. Was it a fox? Was it linked to Siffrin? I had caught the scent of a young fox on the air and heard the chilling *click-click-click* of claws.

"But why?" I asked. "What do you want?"

The dog spoke slowly, as though I was a fool. "I already told you—one of the Elders sent me. I need to find your brother. I thought you might lead me to him."

"Pirie?" I gasped.

He went on as though I hadn't spoken. "I never thought I'd have to walk about the Graylands aimlessly. The air here is *poison*—Canista can only guess what it's doing to my coat." He glanced at a wiry brown forepaw.

"Your coat . . . it looks filthy."

His eyes grew wide. "My *real* coat. I told you, I'm in wa'akkir. I've taken on another shape. Don't you understand?"

"That's . . ." I didn't know what to say. "It's impossible. No one can change that much. A fox is, well, *different* from a dog . . . Take a look at yourself! You could never pass for a fox."

"Does *anyone* really look at themselves?" he asked through narrowed eyes. I didn't know how to respond. "Just forget it," he snapped. "Forget you ever saw me." He made to step around me, but I blocked his path.

"No way!" I rose to my full height. "I want to know what this has to do with Pirie. I don't understand who sent you. Was it that nasty vixen with one gray eye, the fox who came to my family's den?"

I thought I saw the small dog shudder. He dropped his gaze, pushing past me. "You don't know anything."

A shot of anger ripped through me. I spun around and bit him hard on his wiry tail. The dog yelped in surprise.

"You idiot!" he spat. But instead of turning on me, he broke away, tearing down the deathway between the shimmering buildings.

I started after the dog, but he was quicker. By the time I'd reached the end of the buildings, he was nowhere to be seen. "Come back!" I howled into the night. "I need to know what you want with my brother!"

There was a scuffling of paws along the edge of the deathway. A creature was shifting in the pool of darkness beneath a broken brightglobe.

"Siffrin . . . ?" I murmured, my confidence waning.

One black paw stepped into the light. A pretty fox cub trod toward me. Her ginger fur looked soft and fuzzy; her muzzle was short; her brush was slim.

"Isla?" she whispered.

I stumbled away from the cub as if struck. Dizzying rage hammered through my body. It clenched at my throat like powerful jaws, so taut that I could hardly breathe. I found myself staggering, lurching sideways. Sickness rose inside me, acid and urgent. I retched and heaved as my legs collapsed beneath me. The sickness came in violent spasms, infinite beetles pouring onto the ground.

When I looked up, the little fox was in the same place, her whiskers twitching with concern. Her eyes were wide and innocent, but beyond their bronze light there was something knowing.

Something that couldn't be trusted.

6

"It's all right, Isla." The fox cub looked down on me, her eyes full of pity. "Don't be afraid."

"I'm not afraid!" My words came out as a strangled cough. I spat out more beetle gunk, giddy and breathless. Anger bubbled inside me. I lunged toward the cub, but I crumpled over. What was happening to me? My eyes were streaming and I could hardly see where I was going. Rage clawed at my throat and I gagged again. "I'll kill you!"

The cub started chanting under her breath, but I couldn't make out the words. Spitting the sick from my mouth, I glared at her. She swayed before me—or was I swaying? My mind was playing tricks on me. Her black ears seemed to be growing longer. Her brush shot out and fluffed up behind her. Her legs seemed taller, so much taller . . . I gave my head a shake. I was losing my grip on reality. The fox cub's snout seemed to curve before her, and her ginger fur darkened into red. Nausea gripped me once more and I slumped on my side. My body contorted with cramps and my eyes screwed shut. My breath escaped in spiky rasps.

"Isla . . . Isla . . ."

I reached through the dark spinning sickness. The voice was deeper—it was different. I blinked hard and looked up.

The cub had gone. In her place there was a young male fox with the deepest red coat I had ever seen.

Just as quickly as it had gripped me, the sickness drained away. The cramps loosened and the clamor in my mind grew still. Uncertainly, I looked around, not daring to put my weight on my paws. There was a mound of sick beside me. I drew my face away, back to the beautiful fox.

"You're fine now," he assured me. His brush swished gently above the graystone.

"But . . ."

"Take a few breaths and stand up."

I swallowed with a wince. I could still taste the tang of acid in my throat. Tentatively, I rolled onto my paws. I was standing—I was all right. A moment ago I felt like I'd been tossed in the air by a pack of dogs, but somehow the feeling had passed. I inspected my limbs, sure I must have been injured in the process.

"There's nothing wrong with you, Isla," the young fox assured me.

I started to reply, but only a squeak emerged from my parched throat. I tried again. "How do you know what I'm called?"

The eyes were the most unsettling thing about him. They were the eyes I had seen on the mangy dog, the eyes of the fox cub who'd appeared under the broken brightglobe. He spoke softly. "You told the old fox in the wildway your name last night. I was listening in wa'akkir."

Fear ran along my back and I stepped away from him instinctively. "What is wa'akkir?" I asked in a whisper.

"It isn't safe to talk about it here, in the middle of the deathway." He urged me to follow with a tip of his head, but I stood where I was.

My ears flicked back. "Is it . . . Do you turn into different creatures?"

His voice was so low I could hardly hear him. "It's a foxcraft, an ancient form of shape-shifting. With it I can mimic the appearance of another cub of Canista. I copy what I see, what I feel with my senses. I do not *become* someone else—it just looks that way to the untrained eye."

"The dog . . . ?"

"I saw him at the outskirts of the Graylands—this sorry little creature with dirty fur. What could look more different to my natural form?" He lifted his muzzle pompously, flicking his bright red brush.

I took in the richness of his coat and the black outline of

his eyes. My gaze dropped, strangely embarrassed. He had witnessed my panic in the black dog's yard. He had seen me vomit beetles,

"So this is what you really look like? When you're not in . . ."

"Wa'akkir."

A shiver went through me.

"What about the cub, who was she?"

I felt his gaze boring into me. I lifted my eyes.

"Haven't you guessed?" He didn't wait for a reply. He turned away from me and trotted along the edge of the deathway. I watched him progress over the cool stone ground. As he slipped under a brightglobe, his shadow leaped behind him.

I started to follow.

Siffrin trotted along the bank of the deathway and cut behind some furless dens. I trailed him at a distance, watching the swish of his bushy tail. He had cleared two fences and circled around a cluster of trees before he even threw a glance over his shoulder. What if I hadn't followed him? His certainty that I would rankled me, but I was too bewildered to challenge him. My legs throbbed from running and my throat felt like rats had been fighting in there.

Siffrin rounded the trees and padded toward the side of a furless den. There was a metal rod sticking out of the wall.

Water drizzled from it, splashing onto the graystone and rolling to the nearby grass verge. The young fox dropped his head and lapped at the water with a leisurely air. I stood watching, paralyzed with thirst.

He took his time.

Eventually, he drew back from the metal rod and turned to me. "Drink."

I didn't need to be told. I fell upon the drizzle of water, slurping and snapping, letting it fizzle on my tongue. It tingled against the back of my throat, extinguishing the fire the beetles had left. When I'd finally drunk my fill, I looked around. The fox had vanished. What sort of crazy magic was he using? What was he even—

My thoughts were interrupted by the soft swish of a red tail. Siffrin was standing ahead of me, his ears twitching impatiently. As I started after him he turned away and skirted around the furless den. He scrambled through a gap between neighboring patches to a sort of wildway circled by railings. His muzzle punched the air and his whiskers flexed. He was training his senses—sniffing out the secrets of the night. He must have been satisfied with what he discovered, since he glided between the railings into the wildway.

Where was he leading me?

My legs throbbed with strain. Just when I felt I could go no further, he disappeared behind a bush. His voice floated toward me. "In here."

I nosed my way between the branches. The tiny leaves tickled my whiskers. The inside of the bush was hollow, like a cave. Siffrin stood in the middle, preening his long tail.

I sat opposite him, wishing the space between us was wider. It was a cool night, but under the bush, in Siffrin's presence, it felt airless. I knew Ma and Fa would be worried if they found out I had followed a stranger like this—but I couldn't think what else to do. I thought of Greatma with her wise, whiskery face. If only she was here to guide me.

Siffrin eased himself onto his side with a yawn.

I cleared my throat. "What do you want with my family?"

His eye slid up to meet mine. He paused, running his tongue over his muzzle. "Pirie. I'm only looking for Pirie." He gave his head a shake. "But it's obvious you don't know where he is. I've watched you ambling about the Graylands aimlessly for the better part of two nights."

My ears were flat. "Why do you want Pirie?"

"Jana needs to speak with him."

"The . . . the Elder Fox from the Wildlands?"

He cocked his head in acknowledgment.

Old foxes from the world beyond the Great Snarl wanted to talk to my brother. Not Greatma, not Ma or Fa . . . Just Pirie. A fox cub. "But who are they?"

Siffrin sighed with great emphasis. "Don't you know anything?"

My fur bristled. "I know how to bite a dirty dog on his tail."

His lip twitched, and for a moment I saw the flicker of a sharp white fang. "Be careful, cub. I don't have to help you."

"I didn't think you *were* helping me," I snapped. "Didn't you say you're a messenger of Joona?"

"*Jana*," he sniffed. "The Elders help foxes; I help the Elders. It's all the same." He trailed his eyes over the inside of the bush. "I'm tired. It's been a long night already, what with getting you out of scrapes. Let's get this over with."

I blinked at him.

Again with the slow voice, as though I was stupid. "You can ask about the Elders. I will tell you some of what I know. Don't go on about what Pirie has to do with this, as I really can't answer—I'm just a messenger. I will tell you a bit about foxlore, but don't expect me to teach you any foxcraft."

I tried to ignore his rude manner. "What is foxcraft?"

His bronze eyes were back on my face, staring with ill-concealed distaste. "You really don't know?" He let out his breath slowly. "I pity the urban foxes, kept in the grime of the Graylands." He settled back and his voice grew serious. "Here's what you should have been told, and told again, from the day you were born: of all Canista's cubs, Fox has suffered the most from the cruelty of the furless. Dog longs, more than anything, to fit in. He thrived in the Graylands, digging a comfortable place for himself as servant to the furless. He was fed and cared for, but there were terms to his acceptance. He would live as a prisoner, tethered at the end of a rope. Soon he was so well fed on the spoils of the furless that he forgot all memory of his time in the wild, and he lacked the desire to free himself. He lived in a pack with the furless as his leader. His own will withered like a plant without water.

"Wolf was an ancient and noble creature, the largest and fiercest cub of Canista. He would not be controlled by the furless. He ran to the Snowlands, the frozen realms beyond their reach, where he howled to his ancestors to save him. But in his eagerness to be free, he found himself in a land so brutal that he needed the help of his enemies to stay alive, for a lone wolf cannot feed his cubs. In time, fights emerged between the wolves, battles for the best of the kill, for the warmest place to sleep. The strongest claimed that they were kings and that weaker wolves were their slaves. A system of control emerged, more brutal and no less binding than the furless's imprisonment of Dog. In the end, despite his size and power, Wolf cowered before spirits and bowed to the rule of the pack. Confused and superstitious, he forgot how to survive alone."

I pictured the beast I had seen in the cage on my first night wandering in the Great Snarl. Was he part of a kingdom, a slave that bowed to others?

Siffrin went on. "Only Fox had the courage to live without rules, without the hierarchies of others—to hunt and survive in freedom and peace. For while Wolf and Dog are so brutalized that they will gladly kill their own kind, Fox avoids conflict at all cost. She does not yearn to control others—only to live by her own wits. She does not scare or torture her prey, like a cat—she does not gain pleasure from the chase. For that, she is distrusted by her brutish cousins, the other sons and daughters of Canista. For her independence, she is tormented by the furless. The Graylands are haunted by snatchers, who round up foxes and take them away. Even in the Wildlands the furless hunt us, using dogs and poison to kill us. They shoot us with metal sticks and gas our dens. They give us no peace."

Sadness crept over me and I lowered my muzzle. "I have heard about such things. My greatma told me." I thought of all the foxes who'd been taken unfairly before their time. But Greatma had never mentioned Dog and Wolf—I scarcely thought we were connected to those savage creatures. Yet when the black dog had barked at me, I'd understood her words. When the wolf had cursed me, his bitter rebuke had stung. We were of the same ancestor, long ago.

Fox-ka! Conniving, crafty wretch!

"They hate us because we scavenge and steal," I murmured beneath my breath.

"Steal?" Siffrin's fur puffed defensively. "Occasionally, we may take what we find—what others have abandoned. This is not theft."

I thought of Ma and Fa, who worked so hard every night to find us food. Treading the yards behind furless dens, sniffing out rubbish the furless left behind. My muzzle fell solemnly. "I know."

"It was always hardest for Fox, with so many enemies," said Siffrin. "Did your greatma explain what allowed us to survive—to live free among the furless? To hunt our prey without being seen? To elude our enemies as they circled us? It is foxcraft that saved us. Even you can karak, just about. I heard you throw your voice to the air like a bird. Though your slimmering needs work—the mouse saw you soon enough."

I licked my chops fretfully. He had been watching all that time, though I'd never noticed him. I thought of how I had pursued the mouse, stilling my breath in the hope that the contour of my body would fade from its sight. Is that what Siffrin meant by slimmering? I hadn't realized there was a word for it—I'd thought of it as one of Pirie's tricks. Unlike my brother, I'd never been good at slimmering. Siffrin was right—the mouse had seen me . . . Shame crept along my back and prickled the white hairs at the tip of my tail. "You must have been quite close to see that."

"My slimmering is better than yours." His eyes glinted with amusement.

Quietly, I was impressed, but I wasn't about to admit it to this arrogant fox. "And you do this shape-shifting—that's a foxcraft?"

"Wa'akkir." He stretched out an elegant black forepaw.

My mind leaped to the old fox I had come upon the previous night.

You come. You ask for Pirie. You go. You come. When will you leave me alone?

The old fox had acted like we'd met before. Perhaps we had . . . "You mimicked me, didn't you? You've been asking after Pirie as though you were his sister!"

"Once or twice," said Siffrin, unapologetic. "I thought it might help me to find him."

I thought of the cub who'd emerged from beneath the broken brightglobe.

"And when I met you as . . . as my double."

Siffrin dropped his gaze. "I wasn't planning to do that, but you left me no choice."

"It was . . ." I struggled to find words to express the horror and rage I'd experienced on meeting myself.

Siffrin drew the white tip of his tail to his muzzle. "The imitated creature should never encounter their double. It is dangerous for the double, who may be attacked. It is . . .

disturbing to see yourself. Even if you don't know it's you, it is unsettling."

Unsettling? It was far worse than that. The reeling sickness, the fury—I could hardly bear to think of it. I might have killed him.

"Jana would be angry with me if she found out," he admitted. "It is against foxlore to confront the one you have imitated in wa'akkir. Because of the dangers, because of how it might make them feel. But you refused to understand. I needed something to jolt your awareness." He ran his tongue over his muzzle. "I didn't realize what a powerful effect it would have. I guess the laws of foxcraft are there for a reason. I won't be breaking them again."

I glared at him. He had known that appearing as my double could harm me, but he'd done it anyway to prove a point. A trickle of the rage I'd felt ran down my throat. I'd have liked to bite him on the tail again.

"The shape-shifting," I began. "Can you show me how to do it?" I sat on my haunches and looked at him hopefully.

"Absolutely not—foxcraft isn't for a cublet like you, particularly wa'akkir. It can be perilous: a fox may be harmed as a double and never return to their own body. To shape-shift, the fox must study their subject, mimicking their movements and behavior. It takes wisdom and maturity." His gaze told me these were things I didn't have.

My ears flicked back. "Do you know what happened to my family, where they might have gone?"

He reached out an elegant foreleg and started to groom himself, speaking between licks. "I don't know anything about that. When I arrived at your den the strange skulk was there."

"And my family had gone?"

Siffrin paused, one ear twisted to the side. "Yes," he murmured gruffly. "Now, if that's all, we should get some rest."

My tail drooped with disappointment. Then I remembered his speech about what I could ask. "Who are the Elders?"

"They are the guardians of foxlore, the wisdom and teachings of foxcraft. They are the seven wisest foxes of the Wildlands."

"And what do they want with Pirie?"

Siffrin sighed. "I already told you—"

"You must have an idea. Couldn't you just—"

"*Silence,*" he hissed.

My jaw tensed at the rebuke. I was about to protest but, quick as a flash, Siffrin was on his paws. He caught my eye and his ears swiveled around. I jumped up too, craning my neck. There was the faintest murmur against the grass. Was that the hush of pawsteps? My ears pricked up, and I started to untangle the sounds of the night. I sensed more than one creature. I counted three, four . . .

A haunting gekker—the cry of a fox—cut through the air. I gasped, cringing against the grainy soil beneath the bush. Siffrin's handsome face was fierce, his lips pulled back and hackles raised.

The voice rose again, just brush-lengths away on the far side of the bush. "The Master has spoken!" a male fox screeched. "The cub must be found!"

A chorus of high-pitched, stuttering gekkers, and I started to tremble. Should we try to run? I looked to Siffrin.

The smallest tilt of his head warned me to stay where I was.

There was a shuffle of paws at the edge of the bush.

And a shriek so close it was almost inside me: "I can smell the cub—the cub is here!"

7

Siffrin snuck to the edge of the hollow inside the bush. He jerked his muzzle. "This way," he mouthed.

I crept to his side.

Another shrill scream pierced the night. "Find the cub!"

There was a scrabble of claws at the edge of the bush. Someone was coming. Siffrin started to nose his way out, moving in the opposite direction. "Stay close to me," he whispered. "We'll have to outrun them." He shuffled silently beneath the branches. I saw his red flanks disappear in a cloud of leaves. Soon only the tip of his white tail remained, and then this too slipped between the branches.

I started to trace Siffrin's steps. A growl rumbled behind me, and I wheeled around to see a fox's head jut through the foliage. His face was covered in dark gray fur. His snout was long and thin, and one of his ears was torn. He glared at me from the far side of the hollow bush, his dark eyes rimmed in scarlet.

The fox's face contorted. "Stay where you are!" he commanded.

My heart thundered in my ears and a tiny whimper escaped my throat. The fox was approaching through the branches, extending a single black paw toward me. The claws were chipped and stained in blood. His fur was mangy, bald in patches, and I saw a pattern like a broken rose near the top of his foreleg. It was just like the one on the tawny fox who had stalked my den with the one-eyed vixen. It ran in dark red grooves over his flesh.

"Isla! This way!" It was Siffrin's voice from the far side of the branches.

I spun around and scrambled through the bush, blinded for a moment by a shower of leaves. For a few beats I was swimming through arching branches, kicking and fighting till I tumbled out onto the grass next to Siffrin.

He started to run and I stuck to his side, forgetting the exhaustion in my legs. We broke across the wildway, and I heard pawsteps drumming the earth behind us. I didn't even dare to look.

Siffrin was so quick—I could hardly keep up. Gritting my teeth, I forced myself to go faster.

The foxes charged after us. Their stuttering gekkers struck terror in my heart.

We dived through the railings and out of the wildway. I could hear the foxes on our tails as we broke across the deathway and leaped over fences, slashing a path through the lawns behind furless dens. Siffrin glanced into the sky and over his shoulder. He ran faster, hopping down steps that I only just managed to clear with great bounds. We rushed by a lone furless who gawped at us, passed another who didn't even notice. The deathway split and we followed. A row of trees lined the bank and this gave me hope, but as we sprinted toward them I realized they were too widely spaced—they offered no cover.

The land of the furless was stark and jagged. There was nowhere to hide.

A series of gekkers rose behind us as paws pounded graystone in frenzied pursuit. They were getting closer.

I turned to Siffrin. To my horror, I realized he was slowing down. "What's wrong?" I gasped. "Don't stop, they'll catch us!"

A flash of those eyes and a dark thought seized me: what if this was a trap?

"I had to," he yelped. "You won't outrun them and I can't leave you behind. Jana said . . ." A fleeting look over his shoulder. "Trust me," he urged.

But I trusted no one—Greatma had taught me that. *Trust no one but family, for a fox has no friends.*

Siffrin slowed to a trot, his eyelids quivering. He started to chant under his breath. I caught some of his words: "What was seen is unseen; what was sensed becomes senseless . . ."

At last I dared to look behind us, keeping pace at his side. There were five foxes charging along the bank of the deathway. They would be here in moments, and then . . .

And then . . .

"This way!" growled Siffrin. He rolled on his side in a sudden movement, falling behind one of the trees along the bank. A split-second decision—I would stay with him. I slammed to a halt but I overshot, my legs kicking behind me and my brush flicking up. With a scramble I pounced to Siffrin's side.

But what could he do? The foxes would see us.

"Siffrin?"

His eyelids still fluttered. He hardly seemed aware of me.

"*Siffrin?*" I whined. "They're almost here!"

His eyes flicked open and he took me in. "Don't move!" he hissed, his white teeth flashing. He planted his forepaws on my back and threw me roughly against the graystone. He pinned me down—my muzzle was whiskers away from the tree trunk.

My whole body shook with terror. I tried to fight but he bore down harder, squeezing the breath from my lungs. I should never have gone with this devious fox. The others were coming—were almost upon us—and Siffrin had trapped me, a rat to be slaughtered.

In a low voice he started to chant again. He was pressed so close I could feel his heartbeat. Not wild like mine but slowing down, as though he was resting—almost asleep.

The trunk of the tree was flooding my vision, so that all I could see was its leathery bark. I reached out my forepaws, but he pinned me down harder. I heard the thump of paw-steps. Faintly I felt the foxes draw close, but my senses were drowning as he kept on chanting.

What was seen is unseen; what was sensed becomes senseless . . .

The thrum of my heart in my ears, through my whiskers.

All the while chanting: Siffrin chanting. Time became frosty, my heart thumped slowly. My forepaws were gossamer, finer than moths' wings, like ice on a frozen puddle.

Gradually I became aware that the chanting had stopped. Siffrin released me, falling back against the ground. For an instant I was a mouse freed from a cat: too stunned to move, even to save myself. Carefully I turned my head, taking in my surroundings. The foxes had gone—only Siffrin remained. He had slumped onto his side beneath the tree. I rose to my paws, amazed I wasn't injured. The breath flooded back to my lungs and I felt myself expanding. I sniffed the air, but there was no trace of our pursuers.

I turned to stare at Siffrin but kept my distance. "What happened?"

He didn't reply. I looked at him more closely. His body was trembling and his breath came in shallow pants. His eyes had a dazed look about them.

I peered again over the quiet deathway. There was no one around, not even the furless. I could run now and escape him—he was in no state to follow me. I started a few paces down the deathway. I thought of how Siffrin had the chance to hurt me, but here I was, without a bruise. He could have outrun the other foxes, but he'd stopped because I couldn't keep up.

My muzzle crinkled with confusion. I looked over my shoulder. Siffrin was still lying on his side.

I padded back to him. "Are you . . . all right?"

Slowly his dull eyes roved toward me. He blinked twice, as though trying to focus. "It worked," he muttered. A raking cough shuddered through him. His whiskers pulsed. "They've really gone?"

I cocked my head. "They've gone," I told him. "Why didn't they catch us?"

There was a sly twinkle in Siffrin's eyes, though his breath still came in heaving gasps. "I slimmered," he managed. "Like when you tried to catch the mouse. They must have run past, unable to see us. I threw a pelt of quiet over you, so it covered us both. I didn't know if I could do it, I just . . ."

He coughed again and reached out his paws. He tried to rise and fell back onto his belly. He gritted his teeth and tried again.

I watched him, perplexed. "Did they hurt you?"

Siffrin was standing now, with great effort. He moved gingerly, placing one paw in front of another. "They didn't touch me. They can't have seen either of us or we'd be dead."

My ears twisted. "So what happened to you?"

He caught my eye. "It's my maa . . . It's been a long day and all that wa'akkir, it drains a fox. Now the slimmering . . . I just need to rest a while. By sunrise I'll be fine."

I didn't know what he meant by "maa," but it wasn't the right time to ask. I followed him as he hobbled along the bank of the deathway. He crossed into the yard of a furless den. There was a wooden building at the end. The entrance was ajar and we peered inside. I noticed lots of strange objects—shiny containers, paw covers I'd seen the furless use, and the metal frames with wheels that they sometimes spun about on, propelling themselves around the Great Snarl. Siffrin entered and I paused behind him, sniffing. It was quiet and a little damp inside the wooden building. I doubted any furless had been inside for a long time.

Siffrin slunk beneath the metal objects with the large round wheels. He reached the far corner of the wooden den and sank to the ground with a sigh. "Five foxes were following us. You saw one up close, I think?" His voice sounded weak, a little frail, like Greatma's.

I stood next to one great wheel, unwilling to follow him further into the wooden building. He may have saved our lives, but there was something about Siffrin that made me nervous. "I don't think they're the same foxes I saw at my family's den," I murmured with a shudder.

"The gray-faced one—did you look into his eyes? Were they red?" Siffrin pressed.

I thought a moment. I remembered the haunting face that had burst through the bush and snarled at me. His long snout was pointed—his wide eyes had been etched in scarlet. "Maybe. A bit red, anyway."

"The Taken," Siffrin breathed. "They must be part of Karka's skulk."

A chill ran down my back—I'd heard that name before. "You mean the one-eyed fox who was at my den?"

He lowered his head onto his paws. "She commands them, in a way." His ears flicked back. "It's lucky that she wasn't with those foxes tonight."

"What does she want with me?" I asked. I didn't care about Siffrin's rules—ask this, answer that. Those foxes might have killed me. I was entitled to know why.

His reply bore none of his earlier arrogance. "I'm not sure. Karka may be after Pirie. It probably has nothing to do with you. She'll be following you in order to reach him."

I bristled. "It has everything to do with me! Pirie is my brother."

Siffrin looked at me wearily. "Either she is using you to find him, like I tried to. Or . . ." He frowned. "You were born so early, long before malinta. It is strange to see a cub before the first buds form in the trees. I've never heard of such a thing." He became quiet, his bronze eyes thoughtful as he drew his thick red brush about him.

"Or what?" I prompted.

Siffrin's lids drooped over his eyes and he let out a long breath. His head rolled slightly to one side, resting on his forepaws. In moments he was sleeping, his chest rising and falling without a sound.

I longed to know what had happened to Pirie, and why other foxes were looking for him. I thought of waking Siffrin up, but he seemed so worn out, I wasn't sure I dared. A deep tiredness was also gnawing at my body. Seeing him dozing so peacefully, I yearned for sleep. I padded along the wall of the den and climbed behind the open door, beneath dangling cobwebs by the pile of old furless paw covers. I chewed absently at one of them, watching Siffrin for a while. Whatever his reasons, he had saved my life and had hurt himself in the process—in a way I couldn't understand. So perhaps he wasn't all that bad. Yet a nagging voice ate away at me as I stared at the handsome young fox, warning me to be careful. Who were the Elders? What did everyone want with Pirie?

Why did this fox have so many secrets?

He had said he'd be fine when sunrise came. But as dawn broke over the Great Snarl, Siffrin stayed curled in a ball, his chest rising and falling quietly. He slept on as the rumble of manglers filled the air. He did not stir when songbirds trilled and sirens howled along the deathway.

As the clacks and barks of the furless drifted from their nearby dens, Siffrin did not wake up.

8

It wasn't until dusk that Siffrin's eyelids flickered and he stretched his long legs. He looked about and found me watching him from across the wooden den. Then he peered through the open door and seemed surprised.

"Did I sleep all day?"

My ears swiveled forward. "Foxcraft must be tiring."

He'd looked so peaceful, I hadn't wanted to wake him. In sleep, the tension had eased at his forehead and the sour tightness relaxed at his muzzle.

I envied him his rest. As the Great Snarl had bustled, I'd tried to sleep too, but every time I shut my eyes I pictured the great furless with the wings of a bird, standing in the center of a huge stone yard—the one I'd seen before in a dream. I felt myself staggering toward her, gazing up at her unfolding wings. Close up, I could see she was carved of rock. She gazed down at me with round, dead eyes.

I didn't like to remember the winged furless. It made a chill run down my neck and a cramp bite my flank.

Foolish foxlet, I thought in self-rebuke. *Why be scared of a furless in a dream?* But the dreams left me uneasy. There was something about her that drew me closer, even though my instincts told me to run.

Siffrin grunted and rolled onto his paws, extending each leg in turn. Then he gave himself a violent shake. As his brilliant red fur settled down he inspected his legs and flanks. "That's better." He looked back at me. "Foxcraft isn't always so draining, but each one has its hazards. And what I tried last night with the slimmering, I hadn't done that before—I didn't know if it was possible. It took a lot of con-centration." He flexed an agile forepaw and smacked his lips. "I'm ravenous. Did you catch anything good to eat?"

My muzzle tensed. While he'd slept I'd prowled the nearby yard for mice. I'd detected one by the verge where the grass grew longer and had tried to trick it by karak-king, throwing my voice into the wind. I'd even attempted Siffrin's eerie chant in an effort to slimmer as he had. But the mouse must have heard me, because it ran away. Instead I'd gobbled up more insects and worms, though I avoided the beetles.

I wasn't about to tell Siffrin that. "You seemed sick—I didn't want to leave you. What if those foxes had returned?"

He gave me a sideways look. "I'd have been fine. They weren't searching for me." He ducked under the large wheels, making for the door. I stepped back as he neared me, careful to keep my distance.

"It's just as well. I buried a cache around here," he said as he trotted past me onto the grass.

"Here? But you don't live here."

He trod along the yard, sniffing the ground. "I've been staying in that den since I came to the Graylands."

I was about to protest—his running the previous night had seemed random, more aimed at eluding our pursuers than finding anywhere in particular.

"It's not so bad," he went on, edging around the side of the den as I followed at a distance. He started digging up dirt with his forepaws. "Of course, nowhere in the Graylands is *nice*—it's all filthy and dusty and it stinks of the deathway. And there's no chance of catching anything as tasty as a rabbit." He paused to glance over his shoulder. "The grime gets everywhere. Urban foxes reek of it without even knowing."

I glanced at my own fur, shame creeping over me. Did I stink? I took a step back toward the side of the wooden den.

Siffrin returned to his digging and gave a yelp of triumph as he swept away a small mound of dirt, revealing the smooth gray pelt of a creature. In spite of myself I crept closer as he tugged two small bodies out of the cache and dropped them on the grass.

They were voles. Hunger churned in my belly. I hadn't seen anything like that since my family had disappeared.

Siffrin laid a brown-feathered bird next to the voles. He tapped its beak with his paw, giving it a sniff before crunching down on a wing. Feathers spun through the air as he gave the bird a shake. He ate for a moment without looking up, shearing off chunks of meat with the jagged teeth at the side of his mouth as his forepaws held the body still. Then he looked at me, and his ears twitched.

"Don't you want any, Graylands cub?"

I took a tentative step forward as Siffrin returned to the bird, slurping and chewing with satisfied growls.

Ears flat, I crept toward him, staying low to the ground. Quickly I snatched up the voles and shrank back. I hurried away with the small bodies in my jaws, carrying them into the wooden den. There, behind the door, I gobbled them down whole.

When I wandered out of the den, my belly full of delicious meat, Siffrin was settled on the grass, washing his paws. He didn't look up when I approached. "We should go," he began.

"Go? Where?" I watched as he flexed his forepaw and vigorously licked it clean of dirt. I glanced at my own paws. There were bits of gray fur on them from the voles.

"We've both been searching for Pirie. The Graylands are vast. We aren't going to find him. But in the meantime, Karka and her skulk may find us. I've been thinking about it. I don't think it's safe for us out here—particularly for you."

I stiffened. "I'm not going to abandon my family because you turn up from the Wildlands and say I should. They're out there somewhere, and I'm going to find them."

He watched me a moment. There was an expression on his face that I could not read. He lowered his gaze.

"Isla, I think you should know—"

"I won't go anywhere without my family—"

We had spoken over each other. Now we both fell silent.

Dusk was transforming to night. A dark pelt swept over the sky, which grew fuzzy with the glimmer of brightglobes. I cleared my throat. "I can't leave the Graylands."

He didn't meet my eye. When he spoke, his voice was gentler than I'd ever heard it before. "Isla . . . It isn't safe for you here. There's no point circling the deathway without a plan."

"I'm not going to circle it, not any longer. I want to go home." When Siffrin didn't respond, my voice grew louder. "You understand, don't you? Without my family I have nothing. Ma, Fa, Greatma, and Pirie—those foxes are my entire world. I've learned a lot about the Snarl since I've been out on my own, but now all I want is to return to my den. I don't have anywhere else to go." I felt ashamed at the hint of a whine in my words.

Siffrin drew his puffy tail toward himself and started washing it with firm licks. I couldn't help but watch his technique. He was cleaner than a cat. "I know you want to find them. I understand . . . But there's no point returning to your den," he murmured. "Your family isn't there."

"How can you be so sure? They could have come back."

"I don't think so . . ." His eyes slid to mine, the bronze catching the low light. Then he returned his attention to his bushy tail.

I frowned. Did Siffrin know more than he was making out? "Who is this fox, Karka, the one-eyed vixen? You never explained what she wants with me."

"It's Pirie she's after, but I don't know why. Jana doesn't tell me everything." He ran his tongue over his lips, but he didn't look up.

A bird started warbling in a nearby tree. My ears swiveled around as I watched it hop from branch to branch. "Last night you said . . ." I thought a moment. "You said that Karka commanded those foxes, the ones that chased us— you used a special name for them?"

"Maybe I did," he murmured, noncommittal. "I was tired last night. I wasn't thinking straight." He nibbled at the fur on his back, flexing his neck. "I'll take you to Jana. She can answer your questions. She is wise. She'll know what to do."

My ears pricked up. "Will she help me find my family?"

Siffrin threw me a sideways look. "I don't think you should be focusing on them, not now. You should be . . . looking out for yourself." He seemed troubled, almost sympathetic.

I began to protest. "I'm not going to just forget about them!"

Siffrin drew a deep breath and his voice hardened. "Jana is a very busy fox. You wouldn't want to bother her with minor troubles. The Elders have their own problems, which are larger and more challenging than a cub from the Graylands could imagine." That superior lilt had reentered his voice as he stretched out a forepaw, inspecting the pad. "I don't expect you to understand, but two of the seven did not appear at the last gloaming. One is the legendary Black Fox. If he is missing, if he really has gone, it will be bad for everyone."

I balked at his words. *Minor troubles.* I tried not to listen to the rest of what he said. He hardly deserved my attention, that arrogant, thoughtless fox! Why couldn't he have stayed asleep? I'd liked him better then.

My eyes trailed over the dark yard. A moth was flitting on the evening air. I considered chasing it but resisted the impulse—Siffrin was bound to mock me, particularly if it got away. Despite my effort to ignore him, my mind drifted back to the Elder he'd mentioned.

The Black Fox.

The downy fur at the base of my ears was tingly. I couldn't help it—I was intrigued. "What's so special about this missing fox?" I asked.

A long, skinny insect with countless legs was scuttling across the earth between the grass stems. I batted at it absently. "I thought foxes were always red or ginger?" I remembered Pirie's mottled coat, which echoed Greatma's. "Or gold or gray."

Siffrin sighed irritably. "Now you're telling me you've never heard of the Black Fox? You really are impossibly ignorant, cub." He gave me a hard look. "And I told you that *two* Elders didn't appear at the last gathering. The Black Fox and one other."

"Well, I'm sorry he's missing," I said, not sounding sorry at all. *Rude fox,* I thought. *How dare he call me ignorant?* If I hadn't heard of the Elders, I was hardly likely to have heard of one of them in particular, black, red, or otherwise. I glared at Siffrin, rising to my full height, which admittedly wasn't any larger than a cat. "I mean *they.* I'm sorry *they* are missing."

"You should be," said Siffrin, an edge to his voice. "The Black Fox is the title given to the wisest of our kind in any age—he is the ultimate master of foxcraft. We need him with everything that's happening in the Wildlands. All Elders should be coming to the gatherings. Jana is very concerned."

My tail was flicking a little in the breeze. On impulse I spun around to catch it, but it slipped from my grasp.

Siffrin dropped his own brush and snarled at me. "You're not even listening to me, cub! What I'm telling you is important. It's part of the story of Fox—part of a battle that started the day our first ancestor was born, a battle that will rage until the bitter end."

"Sounds tough," I muttered, settling down on the grass. "But I can't worry about what your Elders are up to. My family has disappeared—I have more important things to think about."

He looked at my tail pointedly. "Clearly." One of his ears twitched. "I don't suppose there's any use in explaining that the affairs of the Elders affect you? They touch all foxes. The Elders are the keepers of foxlore—what they do matters."

I yawned. It was totally dark now—or as dark as the Great Snarl ever got. I started to pad along the yard. There was no reason to stay with Siffrin any longer. I needed to be out on the deathway, where I had a chance of picking up Ma's scent or spotting Pirie's mottled brush.

"Where are you going, cublet?"

"To find my family."

"Wait a moment!" he called.

I turned, my muzzle set. "What is it?"

"Don't go back to your den. It isn't safe. Karka's skulk may still be watching it."

I didn't answer immediately. The truth was, I doubted I could find my way back there anyway. I had crossed so much of the Snarl since leaving our patch, I had no idea where I was. "I'm not going to the den."

"Are you really intending to walk the deathway until you find them? You don't even know where to begin."

He had a point. "But . . . I have to start somewhere."

That cool gaze again. "Don't you realize how huge the Graylands are? And the whole place is teeming. You could follow the deathway from malinta to the gloaming and never pass the same furless twice."

I didn't know what he meant by "malinta" or "gloaming," terms I'd heard him use before. He'd only mock me again if I asked what they were, and I understood his meaning well enough: the Great Snarl was enormous. Didn't he think I'd worked that out for myself by now? But I had to look for my family—what else could I do?

Siffrin rolled onto his paws. "You're a cub on your own, don't you get that? You're easy prey for any passing dog or furless who wants to hurt you for fun. Even our own kind can't be trusted with an unfamiliar cub. And all the time you risk harm on the deathway. That's assuming you find enough bugs to eat."

I glared at him. He would never let me forget about the beetles—any opportunity to ridicule me. "I'm hardly a newborn. I'm almost grown up! I haven't touched milk for at least half a moon."

Siffrin ignored me as he finished his speech. "Even if you eat enough, your chances of survival can't be good. Karka will try to hunt you down. I must have seen a dozen foxes in her skulk. Each will be committed to finding you and your brother. Do you really want to risk another encounter? Without me, the foxes would have caught you last night— and I only tricked them because they can't grasp foxcraft. If Karka had been there, we'd both be dead."

The thought of the one-eyed vixen set my fur on end. "Why do you care what happens to me?"

"I don't," snapped Siffrin. "This isn't about you. Jana told me to find your brother. Since Pirie has vanished, I should bring you to her."

My ears were flat. "He hasn't *vanished*! He's out there with my family. They'll be looking for me." I thrust out my muzzle. "I don't care how long it takes, or if I die trying. I'm going to search every bit of the Great Snarl, what you call the Graylands."

That strange expression crossed Siffrin's face, a tightening at the muzzle, a lowering of the ears. A softening of the voice. "Isla, please listen—"

But I wasn't ready to hear him; I wasn't going to be discouraged. "I'll dig behind each furless den, hunt every stretch of the deathway. I'll search for every winged furless until I find them."

"What's that?" Siffrin sprang in front of me. He stood lengthways on the grass, blocking my path. His tail began swishing excitedly.

I backed away from him but he stepped closer, his eyes taking on a curious glow. My fur rose in spikes along my neck. I had already learned he was faster than me—I knew all too well he was stronger too. Alarm coursed down my back and my hackles rose.

"Leave me alone," I whined.

Siffrin stayed where he was. "If I'd wanted to hurt you I'd have done it already." His whiskers jittered on his angular muzzle. "What did you say a moment ago?"

My voice was smaller now. "I said . . . I'm not giving up on my family."

"Not that!" His muzzle was so close that I flinched. His eyes explored my face. "The winged furless?"

"Oh . . ." Was that what had agitated him? I dipped my head to avoid his searching gaze. "Just something I've seen in my dreams."

"A female furless with long robes, wings sprouting from her back? Standing alone in a big stone yard?"

My jaw fell slack. Had he read my thoughts? Fear flexed along my whiskers and stiffened my muzzle. "You know . . ." I gasped. "But how?" I couldn't resist looking up at him. "I saw that furless in a dream!"

Siffrin's eyes flashed with a triumphant gleam. "I've seen her too!" he yipped. "She's real, she exists—I passed her on my journey through the Graylands. It is far from here, a good night's travel north. You cannot have glimpsed the furless in the waking world."

The bird had stopped chirping. It flapped from the branch into shadow, and the yard felt deserted. Could a furless really fly? None of the ones I'd seen had wings. I thought of the bird with a quiver of loss. I wished that I could fly away . . . "I don't know what you mean," I whimpered, spinning around and making for the fence. "My dreams are my own. Let me go."

"Don't run," Siffrin urged. "You should not be afraid. Maybe Pirie . . ." he faltered, and I turned to face him. His long ears pointed sideways and his tail still swished. "You're of the same litter?"

I cocked my head, but my legs were tensed to run.

"I have heard of a rare foxcraft called gerra-sharm. There are few who can perform it—it is one of the forgotten arts. You are close to your brother?"

Despite my alarm, my chest filled with pride. "We could hardly be closer. Until my family disappeared we slept side by side every day of our lives. We ate together, played together. I was never without him." A twinge at my throat. "I should be with him now."

"This furless with wings," said Siffrin. "She could be important."

"But I've never laid eyes on her, not in real life. You said it yourself, she's too far away."

"There are ways of seeing that require no voyage. They are rare, as I said. But when foxes are so close it's as though they share a single heart, their thoughts can occasionally interweave, like the branches of trees that have grown side by side. A thing may be felt through the mind of another."

Heat pulsed at my throat. I sank low to the ground, my ears tingling. What the red fox was saying could not be true.

"Because you are so close to your brother . . ." Siffrin's tail started swishing as I finished his sentence.

"I saw the furless with Pirie's eyes."

9

A light flicked on in a nearby building. Caught in its haze, Siffrin's red hairs glowed like burning embers. I hunkered low to the ground, wondering if this fox was right about my brother. Had Pirie really crossed the Great Snarl and seen the giant, winged furless—the one I had glimpsed in my dream?

Hope prickled my fur. "Do you think my brother was there?"

Siffrin's tail swept over the grass to rest at his side. "I don't know how else to explain what you saw."

It seemed unthinkable that a dream could reveal my brother's location: crazy to imagine I might find my family if I sought out the winged furless. But I remembered what Fa had said—that he'd left his home in the Wildlands because he'd pictured Ma in his sleep.

Dreams are the beginning.

My heart lurched with excitement and my tail beat the ground, *thump-thump-thump.* "I must go!" I yipped. "He may still be close. I dreamed of the furless in my last sleep."

"The stone courtyard is on the way out of the Graylands. If we don't find Pirie, we will carry on to the Wildlands, and I'll take you to Jana."

My lip twitched. I *would* find Pirie. "Can you tell me where exactly? I needn't bother you any more, I'm sure you're busy. All that . . . foxlore." I didn't like the way he was taking over, telling me what we were going to do. It was *my* family who'd gone missing, and my responsibility to find them.

Siffrin's right ear flopped and he looked slightly miffed. "I am not an Elder. *They* are the keepers of foxlore. I'm only a messenger." His brush rose over the grass. He swept it over the long stems irritably. "It's better that I guide you. The night is full of perils. You can't even catch a mouse. How do you expect to protect yourself?"

"I can look after myself just fine." My voice was cool.

I stepped away toward the wooden den, avoiding his glare. I wondered if there was any way I could guess the location of the winged furless without his help. I tried to remember the vision from my dream, but my memory was edged in shadow.

Fear tightened at my haunches and a twinge of pain gripped my flank.

There were foxes around me; their fur smelled of cinders. I couldn't escape.

"What is it?" Siffrin was peering at me, his head cocked to one side.

I must have cried out.

He watched as I gave myself a little shake and turned to sniff my flank. Carefully I raised my hind leg, stretching it behind me. "I'm fine . . . but when I think of the stone furless in the big yard, I don't feel well. Like something bad happened there." What if Pirie was hurt? Fear crept along my back. The smell of cinders . . . It was the scent of Karka's skulk.

Siffrin's muzzle tightened. "But you still see her? The winged furless? You can picture the courtyard as though you are there?"

I gave a small yip.

"Well, Pirie may be in trouble . . . but he must still be alive."

My ears flicked forward. "Do you really believe that? I wouldn't see the furless if . . ." I couldn't finish. Worry gnawed at my belly as I thought of my brother. Was he out there alone, without Ma, Fa, and Greatma? Had the vicious foxes caught up with him?

"Come on, foxlet." Siffrin padded ahead of me, taking the lead. He started down the path by the side of the furless den. "If Pirie's in danger, we should not waste time."

He was right. All that mattered was finding my family.

I followed Siffrin onto the deathway as he threw furtive glances in both directions. He started creeping along the wall, his red fur dissolving into shadow. A wave of relief rolled along my back, freeing the stress from my haunches. It wasn't just that he could lead me to the courtyard with the stone furless. I would never admit it to him, of course, but I felt safer with the red-furred fox around.

As I trailed behind the white tip of his brush, I had to remind myself to be wary.

I had a lingering feeling that he was more than he seemed—that he wasn't telling me all he knew. Secrets billowed around me in invisible plumes, distorting my vision just as slimmering confused the eyes.

What was seen is unseen; what was sensed becomes senseless . . .

I wasn't sure I liked the sound of the Elders, with their foxlore and mysterious powers. I remembered Siffrin's warning not to bother Jana with "minor troubles." I watched as he turned a tight bend along the deathway, trotting close to a grizzled old hedge. A crinkle of renewed resentment tightened at my throat. His family was probably safe in the Wildlands. What did he care what happened to mine?

I swallowed down my irritation. I had little choice but to stay with Siffrin; he was the only one who could take me to the courtyard. But a plan was hatching inside me. When we reached the stone furless, I'd find Pirie and the rest of my family. I would not allow Siffrin to take my brother to the Wildlands. I ran my tongue over my teeth, feeling the sharp edge of my pointed fangs. Perhaps alone I was no match for Siffrin—but with my family by my side, I was invincible.

I thought of the way Fa licked my ears.

Felt the touch of Ma's nose on my muzzle.

I owed my family everything, and the Elders nothing.

We wound beneath the lights of the Great Snarl. Siffrin paused regularly to sniff the air. He led us off the bustling alleyways—where the furless gathered to cluck and feed—along the dim tributaries of the deathway, where fewer furless could be found.

"Dog!" he growled under his breath. We scrambled into a nearby wildway. Concealed behind twining foliage, Siffrin froze. I copied him, paws fixed to the ground as my eyes searched the deathway for the dog. Two furless yipped to each other, pausing some brush-lengths away. They didn't see us in the foliage and couldn't have smelled us with their dull senses. After a few moments they walked away.

I turned to Siffrin with a curious glance, but his eyes were fixed on the bend in the deathway. A creature was weaving through the wildway behind us, maybe a rat. It was actually coming toward us, its little paws beating a path through the grass. Siffrin did not turn. I followed his gaze to the corner of the deathway. There was nothing there, just graystone. A beat later a fluffy white dog appeared. A furless was walking at the dog's side. She controlled his pace with a rope noosed about his neck. Instead of struggling to free himself, the dog seemed content as he trotted at the furless's flank. They passed on the far bank without sparing us a glance.

Siffrin's shoulders relaxed. He started tracking the edge of the wildway and nosing between the railings.

"How did you know the dog was coming?" I asked. "He wasn't even here yet."

Siffrin lapped his muzzle with his tongue. "I picked up his scent. The night is full of clues, if you know where to find them."

Secretly, I was impressed. I tried to look closer, to sniff deeper. The acid whiff of the deathway disturbed my senses.

We walked through the night. There was a new determination about Siffrin—an unwillingness to pause or explain. He led me through a deserted lot, past row upon row of sleeping manglers. We did not rest. Siffrin traced the border of the deathway but edged around it, slipping unseen over steps, between railings, under fences, through hedges, over graystone that expanded in every direction. Occasionally he paused, his head raised and his muzzle pulsing. His ears rotated and his lips parted a fraction. With a lap of his tongue against his nose, he sniffed the air. What did he smell beneath the breath of the Snarl? What did he sense that I could not see?

As the moon drifted low and began to set, my paws grew weary with fatigue. Siffrin kept trotting forward, pausing with nervous glances as I struggled to catch up. He stood at the edge of a silent stretch of the deathway, gazing into the murky sky.

"I need to stop a while," I told him as I reached his side, breaking the silence that had swelled between us.

Siffrin's eyes drifted down, taking in the deathway. "A little further. I'd like to keep going." He seemed distracted as his brush patted the graystone.

I inspected the pad of one of my forepaws. It was rough and sore. "Is something wrong?"

"No," he said quickly. "It's just . . ." He sniffed again, his brush rising behind him. "This way."

I was about to protest when I saw he was leading me under a sleeping mangler. There was a cat down there, and she scowled when she saw us. She backed away slowly, her eyes wide with challenge. A hiss broke from her mouth and her fur puffed up. She spat as she crept onto the deathway, meowling a nonsense of angry insults.

Once the cat had gone, Siffrin urged me to climb under the mangler. "I'll keep watch," he told me.

I wasn't sure that was necessary, but I wasn't going to argue. I found the patch where the cat had slept. The hard ground was still warm with the imprint of her body. I drew my tail to my flank and fell asleep.

I dreamed of hostile foxes closing in on me, their breath at my muzzle and their haunting gekkers filling the air. They shoved me into a stone yard and I stumbled forward, baffled and afraid. A furless towered ahead of me, her giant wings unfolding.

A whine tore through the air and I sprang to my paws, smacking my head on the belly of the mangler.

"Quickly, Isla!" It was Siffrin's voice. I darted out onto the deathway and he sprang to my side. His eyes were wide with alarm. "I can smell them," he told me. "It's Karka's skulk!"

My heart lurched and I spun around, blinking into the gloom. A strong breeze lashed the narrow deathway. It lifted my fur and tugged at my whiskers.

"The wind is rising," said Siffrin. "It must be angry, with nowhere to go. It's looping around the bends in the deathway, chasing its tail."

Siffrin's meaning struck me like a cat's swipe: the wind was whipping itself in circles. If they hadn't already, Karka's foxes would soon smell us.

"The Graylands are a maze," he whispered. "Sounds are imprisoned; our scents will betray us."

I swallowed the terror that was bubbling inside me. "Can you slimmer again?"

Siffrin's muzzle was rigid. "It won't fool Karka. She will see through the foxcraft—she's the Mage's assassin, she is more skilled than me." His voice was brittle with fear.

"Who's the Mage?" I asked, my paw pads sweating.

"He's the skulk's true leader." Siffrin licked his muzzle distractedly. "I'm not even sure which way to run. The wind in the Graylands deceives the senses . . ."

His confusion surprised me. This was the fox who had sensed a dog was coming even before he'd seen him. My breath came quickly. "We have to try. We can't just wait here to be attacked!"

This seemed to shake him into action. "This way," he hissed, and he broke across the deathway. I sprang after him, trying to grasp at smells. No hint of the foxes found my nose. I remembered how Siffrin had sensed the dog even before he'd turned onto the deathway.

A mangler rumbled alongside us and we shrank into the shadows. When the noxious whiff of the beast had passed, I thought I detected another smell.

"Up ahead!" I yelped. "The foxes are coming."

Siffrin's head whipped around and he drew a deep breath. "No, Isla, I think they're behind us." His brow became furrowed and he sniffed again. "The air is swirling between the tall buildings. It's as though they're coming from everywhere." He started forward again but stopped, uncertain.

The tangy odor of unknown foxes stabbed at my nostrils and snatched at my breath. It was drifting around the bend up ahead. They were rushing downhill toward us.

"Not that way." My chest felt tight as I edged along the bank of the deathway. "Follow me, Siffrin, they're going to catch you!"

But he held back, frozen, his ears twitching wildly. He called to me in an urgent breath. "I don't know, Isla . . . I think you're wrong." A wobble of doubt had crept into his voice. "You need to stick near me or my foxcraft won't protect you."

Another sniff of the foxes approaching. "You said that wouldn't fool Karka anyway!" I could smell the charred remains of fire—the acrid tang that had eddied through my den, that now clung onto the foxes' fur. "Hurry," I yelped. "They're almost here!"

He wavered a moment, his muzzle pulsing. His eyes shot toward me, his tail straight behind him. A shadow was tumbling around the corner. I caught the outline of pointed ears. The skulk blended into a single beast, grotesque as it spilled over the graystone. It sluiced toward Siffrin like pools of dark water.

"Watch out!" I barked as they came into view: five large foxes, their hackles raised. They started to run as they caught sight of Siffrin. I'd been right about the wind—they were heading downhill, just brush-lengths away from where Siffrin was standing. Their piercing gekkers sliced the air.

I recognized the fox with the long snout and the gray face, the one who had glared through the hedge. The rose-shaped scar on his foreleg looked scorched in the light of a brightglobe. The fox scanned the deathway, his small eyes ringed with red. He seemed to be their leader. "Get the cub!" he howled when he spotted me.

"Run!" barked Siffrin over the gekkers. He squared his shoulders and extended his brush, blocking the foxes from going further. I could see the whites of his eyes. "Run away from here, Isla, as far you can!"

The gray-faced fox pressed back on his haunches, preparing to pounce. His claws were outstretched and his fangs were bared.

Siffrin wasn't even facing his way! His startled eyes still stared at me, but they'd taken on a faraway look. His lips were moving, whiskers trembling, whispering words I could not hear. Siffrin dodged as the lean fox sprang at him, rolling in a flurry of spinning fur, reappearing as Karka, thickset and one-eyed.

Wa'akkir, I realized—the shape-shifting foxcraft. The ash-tinged foxes fell back with a gasp. Siffrin slammed against one with Karka's broad shoulder, winding another with her thumping back legs.

The gray-faced fox shook his thin head. His eyes became slits. He dropped his gaze, looking down at Siffrin's paws. "I know what you're doing. I know who you are! Don't pretend you're any different from us." He charged at Siffrin, who was still disguised as Karka. A brown-furred fox rushed to his side. I heard the scrape of their claws as they scrambled on stone, and I craned to see what was going on. With a snarl Siffrin broke free, this time in the form of the mongrel dog. He vaulted into the air, at least a full brush-length, slamming down on the fox that was snapping at his paws. He sent her tumbling onto the deathway.

But two more foxes were pounding toward him.

I watched, transfixed, unable to run. Instead I felt myself drawing closer, a thumping terror in my chest. I could not allow Siffrin to do this alone.

The foxes were pinning him, snapping at his ankles. I heard his cry as he shifted back to his own form. His long red brush was bent behind him as a sandy fox bit down on his neck.

"Stop it!" I howled as I ran at the fox, throwing my weight against her flank. As her fur pressed back I glimpsed the mark of the rose, just like the one on the tawny vixen. And on the gray-faced fox.

What does it mean?

I sank my fangs into the fox's flank. Her fur was ash and cinder—there was something rotten beneath her skin. She gave a yelp and let go of Siffrin. But the brown fox was back, all claws and teeth. He lunged, fangs bared, at Siffrin's legs. I scrambled beneath the brown fox, hugging his girth with my forepaws. I buried my teeth in his soft underbelly, harder and harder through the filthy dead flesh. The brown fox howled and fought to escape me, and I fell away with a mouthful of fur.

The gray-faced fox was standing erect. His eyes bore through me as his muzzle wrinkled. "Catch the cub!" he shrieked as he tensed to attack.

A flash of bloodstained jaws. The sandy fox had started toward me, but Siffrin leaped to block her path. In a heart-beat the brown fox had spun on his haunches, his bloodshot eyes expressionless. There it was, just like the others: the dark red scar at the top of his foreleg.

They all have the mark of the rose.

The brown fox shoved past Siffrin, storming straight at me.

I braced myself. *I won't let him beat me!*

I promised myself I would give him a fight. He dived at my throat and I slipped from his clutches. He lunged again,

118

his muzzle contorted. His forepaws crashed against my chest and he thrust me hard against the wall. My head struck the stone with a mighty thud. Pain pierced through my eyes, my vision blurring red as dark shapes spun around me.

"Isla!" howled Siffrin. "Hold on, I'm coming!" I watched faintly as he fought and tussled. He pounced on the fox who was pinning me down.

Brown against red, their bodies collided.

The voice of the gray-faced fox, fierce and shrill: "You belong to him! Darklands fox, deceitful fox! How dare you fight us, you filthy defector . . . We have seen the mark!"

Siffrin was rising in smooth silhouette—his elegant muzzle, his cloud of red tail. "What can be done can be undone," he growled. "I belong to no one!"

The foxes converged on him, circling and striking. Siffrin darted and swooped like a bird in flight. He pounced higher than them, dived down faster than they could. His hind legs kicked backward as he cut through the air. He mimicked the cawing of crows at dusk—their angry cries seemed to fall from the clouds, swirling and crashing around the foxes in a storm.

For a beat he was gone, a slimmer of nothing.

In an instant: a dog, a fox, just air.

Siffrin fought wildly against his attackers. He twirled and pounced to my beating pulse. They scattered in terror as he seemed to expand, red against black without moon or sun. Then another shape emerged through my pulsing vision.

Those long, lean limbs, that long, gray muzzle.

The snarling fox stalked up to Siffrin and leaped at him from behind, wrapping his forepaws around his neck. Siffrin fell with an agonized yowl. The fox was raking the soft fur of his belly. I couldn't move—I couldn't help him. Pain had worried a path through the back of my head.

It seared through my throat.

It blackened my vision.

Sticky and sweet on my tongue.

10

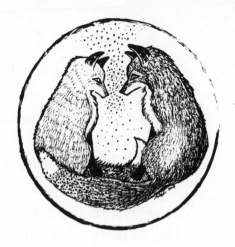

It was early and the grass was heavy with last night's dew. A faint silver light swept over our patch, a halo around the tall den of the furless. I liked this time, before they woke. I drank in the sweet smell of wood bark and earth. The sting of cool air tickled my whiskers.

Our time.

Pirie burst along the fallen branch from the wildway, his fur puffed up and his tail raised behind him. He hopped up and down, spinning tight circles and growling with excitement. "Isla, come quick! There's a *thing* in the grass. I heard it speak!"

My ears rolled back. "There are lots of things in the grass." Fa had brought me an abandoned paw cover, left out in a yard by the furless. I was gnawing on the rubbery base.

It tasted good. There was a satisfying squeak when I bent it beneath my jaw.

"Not like this one!" he said. "Come on, I'll show you!"

He nosed my muzzle and licked my ears. I dropped the paw cover, shoving it closer to the den, where I'd retrieve it later. "Is it the creature with the beautiful voice?" My tail was wagging in anticipation. I'd been seeking out the trilling song for over a moon with no success.

Greatma was watching us from the entrance of the den. "Where are you going, cubs?"

Pirie gamboled up to her. "There's a *thing*, Greatma, a thing in the wildway. I want to show Isla!" He turned to me. "It's not the creature with the beautiful voice. It isn't singing, or I wouldn't call it that, it's . . . Oh, you'll see!"

Greatma's face was stern. "You should stay here, by the den. I don't want you running into cats on your own."

"Ma's in the wildway," I pointed out. "Pirie was just there, isn't that right?"

"Oh yes!" he yipped obligingly.

We both set our most pleading faces at Greatma. Her tufty muzzle trembled and I knew she'd let us go.

"Stay close to your ma," she called as we scrambled over the fallen branch.

Pirie stalked through the twisting grasses of the wildway, pausing, head craned and ears perking up. I mimicked his movements, ears pricked, tail low. The grass in the wildway was much longer than it was at our patch. The clinging dew formed countless speckled lights, catching the shimmer of the dawn on its stems. It dampened my pelt as I slipped between the grass.

"There," hissed Pirie under his breath.

I strained my ears. I caught a husky croak—the oddest sound I'd ever heard. "What is it?" I mouthed.

We stalked closer, stopping as the creature croaked again. It wasn't running away. We circled some shrubs with our whiskers flexed forward. Its croak was surprisingly loud on the crisp morning air—could a small creature really have made that sound? But it had to be small. It hunched beneath us, rumbling between a clutch of tall vines.

Tentatively, I outstretched my paw and pinned back the vines as Pirie crouched by my side. What I revealed was a damp green ball—a clammy creature not much larger than a fox's paw. I held onto the vines as Pirie eased forward, lowering his muzzle to take a sniff. From nowhere, the green ball sprang into the air, trailing legs much longer than its body. It arched over our heads and our ears flicked back.

So high! So quick!

What a strange thing it was, with no tail at all and that loud, croaky voice.

"There you are, cubs." Ma was padding toward us. She dropped the drooping body of a mouse on the grass. All thoughts of the green thing were quickly forgotten as we wrestled the still-warm body between us, growling and yipping as we shared the kill. When we finished, Ma insisted on cleaning our fur, lapping our noses with her soft pink tongue.

My muzzle was damp. I felt the licks of a tongue cleaning my nose and whiskers. I murmured softly, thinking of mice and mornings in the wildway with Ma and Pirie.

"Isla. Isla, are you all right?"

It wasn't Ma's or Pirie's voice.

A nudge of a nose, a nibble at my whiskers. "Open your eyes. Look at me and I will help you."

The damp grass of the wildway faded and pain rose in its place, grinding at the back of my head and gnawing at my tongue. I didn't want to open my eyes—I wanted to be back in the wildway—but I felt them flicker to life of their own accord. At first I saw Siffrin in shades of scarlet. He was leaning over me, his muzzle taut. His whiskers sprang before me, long and fine as they flexed with tension.

His delicate features were panic-stricken. "Tell me what's wrong. The more I understand, the more I can help."

I blinked and cat claws raked my vision. I tried to swallow but my tongue felt thick. "My head," I rasped. "When I fell backward." My voice was strange to my own ears.

Pinched and croaky, like the creature from the wildway. If only I felt strong enough to jump as it had.

"You must have hit it hard. And you bit your tongue. There's blood." Siffrin licked gently around my mouth and I winced. My tongue felt like it was sliced to strips. "You're going to have to look at me, Isla. Look at me or I can't help."

With a twinge, I raised my snout and peered into his face. It was still etched in red and outlined in black.

He fixed me with an intense gaze. "Try not to blink. This won't hurt—I promise." His long black lashes made his eyes look even larger. There was a gleam in their dark centers I hadn't noticed before. I could feel his gaze tugging at me. The gleam grew brighter and his eyes were deep as pools of water, amber melting into gold. I was conscious that his lips were moving, faintly aware of his murmured words.

"With my touch, I sense you; with my eyes, I heal you. By Canista's Lights, I share what I have; we are knit together and you are whole."

I held his gaze, my body relaxing.

His eyes were glowing orange and yellow. Fine lines deep within them were unfurling like buds, spinning like leaves on the wind. A rich, honeyed warmth washed over me and I sighed. The pain in my head was retreating to a dark place, scuttling like a rat between the shaded tributaries of my mind. I did not blink. I dared not miss a moment of the radiance, the sun that glistered through Siffrin's eyes to mine. My tongue fizzled softly, the thickness lifting. It was almost as though my body was floating, soothed and protected, lighter than air.

With my touch, I sense you; with my eyes, I heal you.

Through beams of bright light I saw a cub wandering lost beneath dozens of shadowy trees. Vines grasped at his whiskers and snatched at his tail, and everywhere there was screeching, hissing, cackling. I witnessed his terror as he called for his ma, felt the sharp claws of his dread bury deep in my chest. The cub was desperate and starving, much smaller and frailer than I was now, his fur still brown; he could scarcely survive alone. When he turned, I saw his foreleg was bleeding. With a pitiful whimper, he sank to the ground, drawing his tail to his chest. I felt the fear and knowledge of the darkness that gripped him. I smelled an acrid stench like sour milk.

The sound of pawsteps crunching over leaves.

An old gray fox with a short, thick tail. She lowered her muzzle and whispered in the cub's ear. She gazed into his eyes and licked the blood from his leg. She stopped at the base of a great red-barked tree and started digging, while all the time she chanted softly.

By Canista's Lights, I share what I have; we are knit together and you are whole.

Her brush curled around him as she led him to her den.

Light glanced through a valley where flowers blossomed. I was high in the clouds where the birds were soaring.

The sun set in glittering orange and violet. The black sky arched above in a velvet pelt. Overhead, in the darkness, Canista's Lights prickled, watching the valley like thoughtful eyes. I was no longer lost and alone beneath trees. I'd discovered a land without fear or hunger.

Siffrin drew back from me and blinked at last. I felt myself released from the power of his gaze, gently floating back to our own world. A golden light still dazzled my vision, but colors were returning. I saw the outline of Siffrin's large ears as he hovered above me. Beyond him I could make out the deathway with its guttering brightglobes, and the manglers reclining along its stone banks.

Siffrin was frowning. "How are you feeling?"

I swallowed a couple of times and moved my neck carefully. The back of my head was throbbing, but it wasn't too bad. "Much better." I rolled onto my paws. I was going to be all right. Dawn was creeping along the edges of buildings. My breath coiled before me in wisps of white mist.

"Take it slowly," Siffrin warned me, stepping back as I pushed up onto my forepaws and extended my hind legs.

I stretched out my paw pads. Now that the clutching pain had released my head, I was remembering flashes of the fight with the foxes. The fur rose on my back as I looked along the quiet deathway.

Siffrin's voice was croaky. "They've gone." He must have guessed my thoughts.

I remembered the way they had set upon him like a pack of crazed dogs. He'd fought back, shifting his shape and throwing his voice. "You scared them away," I murmured in awe.

Somewhere in the Graylands, a siren was bleating. A pack of furless howled in tuneless voices.

Siffrin dropped his head with a modesty I hadn't seen in him before. "Most ran without too much trouble."

I thought of the skinny, gray-faced fox. "What about the one that seemed to be the leader—he attacked you from behind. Did he hurt you?" I took a closer look at Siffrin. I noticed spots of blood on his legs. One of his large black ears was torn.

He tapped a shiny wrapper that had blown into his path. It settled in front of him, tipping from side to side like a leaf. The wind was dropping at last. "I'm fine."

I padded up and down the stone ground, feeling the blood flood back to my limbs. I could hardly believe that the terrible pain in my head had faded. I watched Siffrin from the corner of my eye and tried to remember what had passed between us. My mind had been muddled by thoughts of trees—sunlight, a lost cub, a deep pelt of darkness. "What did you do just now? When you looked at me?"

Siffrin glanced up. His eyes were bronze again, but I saw flecks of gold in them and soft swirls of green. "I gave you maa-sharm, the healing foxcraft. I shared my maa with you."

"Your maa?" I asked, forgetting my promise to disguise my ignorance.

There was no mockery in his response. "Maa is the essence of every fox. It is their life source, the power inside them. It is everything they've seen; it is all they have known. It is who they are." His tail swept over the ground as he spoke. "Your maa was injured when you hit your head. Your tongue was bleeding. You probably bit it as you struck the graystone."

My ears flipped back. I remembered the light that had spilled from his eyes, and the feeling of soaring through the air. "That's why I feel better. You gave your life source to me." This realization rocked me and I sat, feeling dazed.

Siffrin's brush swished back and forth. "No more than I could afford to lose, and even that will return in time. I could see it in your face—your maa was fading." The white tip of his tail quivered. "Jana would be cross if I hadn't tried to help."

I met his gaze and a current shot through me—as though his heat and energy were reaching inside me again.

"It sounds dangerous, offering your life source like that."

"Only if you give too much . . ." There was a quaver in his voice. He ran his tongue over the front of his muzzle. "I felt your maa when I shared mine with you." His whiskers pulsed as he drew his eyes away. He sucked in his breath as he gazed along the deathway. "I'm sorry I got it wrong. The wind confused me. That hasn't happened to me before."

I had never heard him apologize. I found it unsettling. Until tonight, he had always seemed so sure of himself.

His ears rotated. "In the end, the foxes fled. They will run to Karka—she will come for us." He paused, lost in thought.

I remembered what he'd said when the foxes pursued us. "You said they serve another fox. That Karka is the Mage's assassin?"

Siffrin let out a long breath. "So much hatred," he muttered vaguely.

"And it was me they wanted," I whimpered. I remembered the gray-faced fox with the red-ringed eyes.

Get the cub!

That's what he'd shrieked. "Who is the Mage? Why would he want to kill me? I don't know those foxes—I never saw them before they came to my den."

"The one you called the leader, the fox with the gray face, he fought harder than I'd expected for one of his kind. He seemed determined to catch you." Siffrin shook his head with a deep sigh. A trickle of blood ran down his torn ear. A red drop fell onto the graystone. I felt the impulse to go to him and wash the blood away. The dizziness was passing and I stood again, taking a few steps toward him. But he kept his muzzle angled from me, and as I reached his side I lost my nerve.

"What do you mean, 'one of his kind'? You said foxcraft wouldn't fool Karka, but it seemed to confuse the others." I thought of the scar like a broken rose that was etched on each fox's foreleg. My ears flattened as I remembered the smell of embers that clung to their fur. There was something strange about those foxes.

Something rotten beneath the skin.

"Karka is different. She leads the skulk on behalf of the Mage. The rest are . . ." Siffrin shook his head. "I don't know what they are." He scratched at his bleeding ear. "But my foxcraft didn't trick Tarr, the slim fox with the gray face . . . or not for long. It was like he knew what to look out for."

I thought of the gray-faced fox, remembering how he'd narrowed his eyes and dropped his gaze when Siffrin performed wa'akkir. Did that allow him to counter the foxcraft—to see the red fox as he really was? Is that why, unlike the others, he hadn't seemed shocked to see Karka's image? I chewed at a split claw. When Pirie slimmered, I could make out his shape if I blinked fast and hard. Could all foxcraft be disentangled for those who knew its secrets?

There was something else at the back of my mind, something I'd heard through the fog of my pain. Then it came to me. "He seemed to know you. He called you a . . ." I thought for a moment. "A Darklands fox."

A shadow crossed Siffrin's eyes. His ears were flat and I saw him shudder. "I've never met him before. I grew up near marshes, at the edge of the Deep Forest. They call it the Darklands now, but it used to be part of the Wildlands. Perhaps he's from one of the Marshlands skulks. He may have known my family."

I frowned. Had the knock to my head loosened my memory? "But you know his name. You called him Tarr."

Siffrin paused. "I heard the others use it." He started slowly along the deathway. I noticed he was limping. Up close, the bites on his legs looked deep. Tracing my eyes over his coat, I spotted dark grooves beneath his fur like scorch marks.

"What's that?" I asked. "The foxes hurt you . . ."

His brush leaped around him, hugging his body so I couldn't see the wounds. "It's nothing," he said quickly. "An old injury." He quickened his pace along the deathway. "Those foxes mean to catch you—even now, they may be tracking our scents, though I doubt we'll see them in daylight. It's been a long night. We need to find somewhere to hide so we can rest till nightfall."

I still didn't know what was different about those foxes—why their fur smelled of cinders and their eyes were ringed with red. Siffrin looked too weary to answer questions. As I edged alongside him, I saw him wince with strain as he hobbled over the hard ground.

The Great Snarl was growling to life with the sunrise. The noises smothered the sounds of our paws and the hush of our breath on the cold, grimy air. I scarcely remembered what I'd seen in maa-sharm. I had a faint recollection of a cub amid trees, though the images waned in the morning haze.

But I felt different.

Siffrin's maa had awoken a deeper memory—a sense that reached beyond thought or knowledge. Of a light that glowed inside me, brilliant and precious. Even here, in the land of the furless, against palls of gray.

It could not be dimmed.

11

Manglers lurched along the deathway, snarling irritably at one another. I hardly noticed them anymore—they couldn't climb their banks to attack us. Siffrin was more wary, his fur puffing up at their angry barks. Maybe he wasn't used to seeing so many where he came from.

I tried to imagine what the Wildlands looked like. The days were longer there; the nights were darker. I knew that from Fa. He had talked of waterfalls, lakes, and streams, great fields of green and shadowy woods. But I struggled to picture them as my eyes trailed over images of furless faces that gazed down on the deathway from giant boards. Lights flickered and flashed everywhere in the Great Snarl, when the sun was high and in the middle of the night. The buildings shot into the clouds, breathlessly reaching for space and air.

What would the world look like with fewer furless in it?

Siffrin cowered away from a mangler as it sped along a bend in the deathway, even though it was nowhere near him. I followed his gaze. The mangler was large and white with a stubby snout. As it passed I saw that the spy hole at the back was edged with wire. Beyond loomed the face of a terrified fox, his mouth wide open in a scream that was drowned out by the noise of the Snarl.

Why was a fox trapped in a mangler?

My heart leaped. "The snatchers!" I hissed as I ducked down an alleyway. Siffrin sprang after me and we backed against a wall as the white mangler grumbled past.

Siffrin shook his fur. "That was too close . . ." He looked exhausted as he peered along the side of a building. "Let's try down there."

We lapped dew from the grass that sprang up by the graystone and drank from little puddles of dark water at the edge of the deathway. It tasted bitter, of manglers, but it quenched our thirst. We trailed around the back of a building. There was no noise coming from inside, no sign of life. One of the spy holes was open. Siffrin pushed up on his hind legs and peered inside.

"It's quiet." His head poked through the small flap. "I don't think anyone's around." He dropped onto all fours.

"We'll try it," I agreed. There was a large pipe skirting the edge of the building. I propped myself up on it and sprang as high as I could, clasping at the open spy hole with my forepaws. Dangling over it, I could see inside. Right beneath the spy hole was a brown box. Beyond, there was open space and high white walls. My hind quarters swung on the outside of the building and my ears flipped back, thinking how clumsy I must look to Siffrin.

"Do you need help?" he yipped.

"No!" I barked proudly, dragging myself through the open spy hole. With my paws splayed, I launched myself onto the brown box. I landed with a soft thud and hopped onto the floor. It opened into a large, empty area. The floor was blue and fuzzy and reminded me of moss. I padded along it, sniffing the strange, lifeless scent of the building. Dust tickled my nose and I sneezed. I heard a soft whoosh of paws and turned to see Siffrin leap through the spy hole. He cleared the box without touching it and landed on the floor soundlessly. I admired the grace and speed of his body. I thought of the power beneath his thick fur, recalling his leaps and kicks when he'd fought the foxes.

I realized I was staring and tugged my gaze away, making a show of sniffing the ground. "I don't think there are any furless here."

Siffrin's ears swiveled forward. He traced a path along one wall, pausing to taste the air. There was a door at the far side of the room, but it was shut. He turned to me but did not meet my eye. "The air is dank. I don't think the furless have been here for a long time. We should be safe to rest." His brush traced the blue floor as it drifted back and forth. "Karka and her foxes will not find us here, and any furless that arrive will have to come through that entrance. There's no other way. We'll have time to escape through the spy hole."

The snarl of manglers still drifted from the deathway, but inside the building it was quiet.

Siffrin settled against the wall a brush-length from the entrance, as though keeping guard. He started washing the wounds on his legs, ears bent back and pensive, as though I wasn't there. I padded along the far side of the wall and relaxed onto my belly. I pretended to inspect my paws, but secretly I watched him from the corner of my vision. The blood had stopped flowing from his ear and a dark scab had formed. His pelt looked shaggy along his back. Even from a distance, I could tell that the foxes had torn away chunks of his fur. Only his fluffy tail looked the same, with its thick red coat and perfectly white tip.

I ran my tongue over my muzzle. I could hardly feel the spot I had bitten, and the ache at the back of my head was a gentle thrum. I was in a better state than him.

Siffrin paused and looked up, catching me watching him. I dipped my head quickly.

"You should get some sleep," he said.

"I will . . ." I folded my forepaws and stretched out my legs. I was thinking of Tarr, the gray-faced fox, and how he'd addressed Siffrin as though he'd known him. "Why is it called the Darklands—the place you come from?"

Siffrin lowered his hind leg and drew up a foreleg, wincing as he flexed his paw. "The Wildlands are even larger than the Graylands, although they shrink every day as the furless expand their territory. They begin where the sun sets, circling beneath the Snowlands. I come from the marshes in the south, along the border of the Deep Forest. The marshes used to be lush and green, with shallow pools full of tasty eels . . . But they changed a while ago."

"What changed about them?"

I heard him sniff. "You ask a lot of questions."

I gnawed at some mud between my claws, then looked up at Siffrin. "The Darklands is a strange sort of name. It makes me afraid . . ."

His bronze eyes flashed, met mine for an instant. "It should," he said in a low voice. "The local foxes avoid the Deep Forest. They say things fester beneath the branches. There are creatures there that thrive in the shadows who never see Canista's Lights. Few foxes live along its borders. Once there were skulks scattered across the marshes—it was a good place to find rabbits and hares. But those foxes have all gone, one way or another. The forest is growing.

Much of the Marshlands have fallen to swamp. The water is putrid; there are no more eels. Even the rabbits have moved away."

I wondered what could be so bad about the forest that it drove rabbits from their burrows. I had never seen one, but when Fa spoke of them his voice became dreamy. "Do you still have family there?"

Siffrin's ears were flat against his head. "I haven't lived near the Darklands for a long time." There was an edge to his voice that warned me not to ask more about his life.

"Where do the Elders live?" I said instead.

Siffrin tugged a clump of loose fur from his flank and set it on the floor by his side. "They are all from the Wildlands, from different skulks. They gather only rarely at the Elder Rock, a raised shaft in a circle of trees. It lies between the Darklands and the Upper Wildlands, but few who search will find it. I saw it once . . ." He trailed off.

The Wildlands sounded so strange and far away. "Has a fox from the Great Snarl . . . the *Graylands* . . . ever been an Elder? You said that the Elders were the wisest foxes from the Wildlands, but there must be lots of clever foxes here. It isn't easy to survive in the Graylands." I thought of Greatma, who was the wisest fox I'd ever met. She always knew how to sniff out the best kill, and she had a sixth sense for danger.

Siffrin drew his forepaws ahead of him and settled his head upon them. "I doubt it," he murmured.

"But why?" I pressed.

He yawned, revealing neat rows of white teeth. "You are brimming with energy this morning."

I am full of your maa, I thought, but I didn't say so.

I watched as he shut his eyes and his head relaxed. The space between us was so wide and empty. I reclined on my side and flipped onto my belly. I folded a paw over my eyes, but I couldn't get comfortable. It took me a long time to fall asleep.

"We should really begin with karakking, but as you're already just about able to do that we don't need to waste any time."

Just about able? My muzzle wrinkled. Siffrin was standing before me on the blue, fuzzy floor of the quiet building. The light from the spy holes drifted across the far wall. The sun had already reached its highest peak. His eyes had regained their sparkle, and the wounds on his ankles were starting to heal. The scab on his ear gave him a roguish look, an imperfection that marred his fine features.

I flexed my whiskers. "Karakking—you mean, mimicking a bird?"

"Mimicking any creature," he corrected. With his energy, it seemed that some of Siffrin's superior manner had also returned.

"I'm *good* at that." I remembered playing with Pirie in the wildway before my family disappeared. Such an ordinary day. I'd karakked when he chased me, pretending to be a crow. Pirie had encouraged me . . . *I didn't think it was your voice at all. It was coming from nowhere and everywhere . . . It was like the wind was calling, and the earth, and the grass. I didn't know where I was! Then the birdcall stopped and I realized it was you.*

I held Siffrin's gaze. "Pirie said so." *Tell me I'm wrong,* I challenged him with my eyes. Tell me a cub from the Graylands doesn't know anything.

Siffrin cocked his head. "You can karak. Fine. Can we get on with this?"

I lifted my muzzle in acknowledgment.

The red-furred fox continued. "Karakking takes very little maa. I can't think of anything too dangerous in its practice." He gave me a pointed look. "Slimmering is harder."

"Pirie can do it," I said defiantly, waiting for Siffrin to argue with me.

He replied slowly, a distracted look crossing his face. "Yes, I can imagine that . . . If he can do it naturally, without training, he must have a strong intuitive grasp of foxcraft."

I relaxed a little. Siffrin and I would get along much better if he showed my family a little respect.

"Pirie is amazing at slimmering. I need to get better at it . . ." The truth was I couldn't slimmer at all. I didn't want to admit that I hadn't caught anything more challenging than a moth since being out on my own, but I didn't have to—Siffrin had been watching me.

He started to pace along the blue floor. "You will be able to slimmer. Any fox can, given enough practice. You're only struggling because you're young and these things come with experience."

"That time with the mouse by the wall . . . I really tried." My tail twitched with frustration.

Siffrin stopped pacing. "Maybe you were trying too hard. Half the trick is not to focus on it, to let your thoughts unravel."

My ears twitched. How was it supposed to happen if I didn't *think* about it?

I must have looked doubtful. "You can't rush it," he went on. "It is best to focus on your heartbeat, that helps to quiet the mind. If you can't hear your heart, listen harder. Wait until it pulses through you, calm and at peace. Only then should you center on your prey."

He started pacing again. "Slimmering creates an illusion. It's as though a pelt of invisibility covers you. The prey won't see you, at least for a few beats, and in that time you can stalk up to them. Like this." He dropped his belly so he slunk low like a cat, poised with one foreleg raised. His tail drifted behind him as he crept along the blue floor, setting down one paw after another.

His jaws parted. I could hear the *shush* of his breath.

"There is a chant for this foxcraft. You don't have to use it, but it may help."

I watched as he circled the floor very slowly. "Won't the prey hear the chanting?"

"Quietly," he murmured. "What was seen is unseen; what was sensed becomes senseless. What was bone is bending; what was fur is air."

A shiver ran down my spine. I took a step away from him, my tail curling around my flank. Light caught the tips of his hairs. His coat shimmered silver, like frost on grass stems. His chest moved slowly as his breath slowed down. His fur seemed to melt into the light, growing translucent.

His voice repeated the chant in a whisper, the words drawling and spinning in clouds of mist.

What was seen is unseen; what was sensed becomes senseless . . .

My ears rolled back and I stared in wonder as he seemed to fade against the blue floor. I caught glimpses of his outline, but when I turned to look at him directly, the red-furred fox disappeared from view. I could still catch the purr of his voice, but I couldn't place exactly where it was coming from. It seemed to be sloping down the walls and circling the chamber, above me, below me—Siffrin's voice was everywhere. Was this slimmering? I was more disoriented than I'd expected. Was this how the voles had felt when the red fox stalked them?

I spun around, sniffing the air. Siffrin was close, so close I felt his breath on my neck.

What was bone is bending; what was fur is air.

The words echoed in my ears, distorting and twisting inside me.

"Enough!" I whined, panting anxiously. "Where are you?" I trod a tight circle, my gaze vaulting across the empty room.

His voice seemed to tumble from the sky. "It's all an illusion."

I took a deep breath, forcing away my fear. Pirie was much better at slimmering than I was, even if he didn't know the name for what he did. If I could counter Pirie's tricks, I could do the same thing to Siffrin.

I blinked hard in one direction, blinked in another. I caught the outline of Siffrin's long brush as he slunk out of view. I turned, blinked again, catching the glimmer of his body. I couldn't make him out completely, but I saw the light touching his furs and the strange glow of his eyes. With a yip I pounced on him. My forepaws struck the solid wall of his ribs. As we tumbled on the ground he came into view, his fur returning in flecks of red.

He let me pin him to the ground with my forepaws. "You scared me!" I growled, nipping him angrily on the jaw. "What was that, anyway? You were slimmering, but you karakked too—you threw your voice! I wasn't expecting it."

His eyes twinkled. "But you worked it out. You're a fast learner, Isla." That strange shot of warmth when he looked at me. I drew back, dropping my paws on the ground. He panted on his side a moment before sitting upright. "It's tiring, performing two arts at once. It draws on your maa. Never do it for long." He licked his paws and stood with a sigh. "Slimmering is good for catching prey or avoiding dogs, but you should know that other foxes can work out what's happening and counter it by blinking—just as you did. There is also a reversal chant. So don't go thinking that if you slimmer, you're safe."

I knew I should ask him more about the chant, but for a moment my words escaped me. I felt confused by the spell he'd cast on me.

Siffrin was standing less than a brush-length away, waiting for me to say something.

I ran my tongue over my muzzle, Siffrin's words echoing in my mind.

You're a fast learner, Isla.

Perhaps most shocking of all, he had paid me a compliment.

I cleared my throat. "My turn. I want to slimmer."

He tipped his head. "If you're ready, let's do it for real. Who knows, one day slimmering may save your life. Until then . . ."

I watched him warily, my tail low. "Until then what?"

"I want you to catch me a mouse."

12

The flickering of lights.

The growling of manglers.

The deathway buzzed with countless furless. Their land of walls and graystone juddered with movement. The wind swooped restlessly between their buildings; the sun glanced off the glinting spy holes of their dens. And always the gnashing, rumbling, clanking. The song of the Snarl.

We stood by the side of the building down an alleyway, a path so narrow that the deathway didn't venture there, as a world of speed and noise spun by a short distance away. The stench of filth and decay overwhelmed my senses. "Shouldn't we wait till night? When it's quieter? Isn't it safer at nightfall?"

Siffrin cocked his head. "I've been thinking . . . wondering if we should start walking in the days and resting at night. We aren't far from the winged furless now, but we need to keep moving. All of Karka's skulk will be searching for you, desperate to find you . . . They are more likely to be active at night."

My fur prickled along my back as a mangler screeched on the nearby deathway. "But the furless are everywhere during the day. The snatchers are prowling. It's dangerous."

Siffrin was gazing onto the deathway, his hackles raised. "Who scares you more?"

I looked to see if he was teasing me, but his face was grave. I thought of the terrified face of the fox trapped in the snatchers' mangler. With an anxious whine I recalled the one-eyed vixen outside my den. I didn't know how to answer.

"The sooner you learn to slimmer, the safer you'll be."

"But Karka isn't fooled by foxcraft . . . You said so!"

Siffrin tilted his head. "At least you'll have protection from some of her skulk, even if not from her—"

"Or Tarr," I interrupted.

He gave me a stern look. "Slimmering is still an important lesson. You need to be able to catch your own food. There are mice along this path."

I pricked up my ears. How was it possible to hear anything beneath the wails of the Snarl? I strained harder. A mangler rushed by on the deathway. In the moments after it passed, I caught the sound of scurrying paws. My body tensed, instantly alert. I stalked along the wall.

A single, high-pitched squeak.

Siffrin was right—there were mice living in the pipe that ran along the outside of the building.

I examined the pipe. I gave it a light tap with a forepaw. Its hard, thick surface seemed impenetrable.

Siffrin was watching me, head cocked. "Now we just need to wait until one comes out."

My ears fell as I turned my attention back to the pipe. It traveled along the side of the building not high above the ground. Just before it met the deathway the pipe bent, pointing down at the graystone. I edged a little closer. The pipe seemed to be open at that end—that's how the mice must have gotten in. It was far too small for a fox to creep inside.

I padded back to Siffrin, who was standing some brush-lengths away. He must have already spotted the opening. He started to groom his forepaw.

I looked from him to the pipe. "It could take a long time for a mouse to come out."

"It could."

"And we need to reach the winged furless."

"We do."

My tail flicked with agitation. Was he trying to annoy me? "So should we just leave it and start moving?"

Siffrin nibbled at a bit of invisible dirt on his paw. "If you like. Who needs to eat?"

My ears flattened. Now I knew he was goading me. "But it's going to take *ages* to catch a mouse here. As long as they stay in the pipe, we can't reach them."

Siffrin sighed. "You're so impatient, Isla."

My fur bristled. It was just what Pirie always said to me.

The red-furred fox set down his paw. "A meal isn't going to leap into your jaws. Sometimes you need to wait it out."

A memory from the wildway by our old patch. Ma stepping toward me, her muzzle crinkling. "What simple lesson can save a fox's life?"

Watch! Wait! Listen!

I shook out my fur irritably and padded some brushlengths away from him, flopping down onto my belly and watching the pipe. I could feel Siffrin's eyes trailing over me, judging me. I would have to sit and wait now, whatever happened—otherwise, he'd be unbearable.

I listened to the snarls of the deathway. I tried to picture the furless with the great wings. Was Pirie still there? My mind wandered as I gazed at the point where the pipe opened over the graystone. I thought of Fa as a young fox in the Wildlands. Was he from the marshes near the Deep Forest? I didn't think so . . . Why hadn't I asked him more about his time as a cub when I'd had the chance?

The scrabble of tiny claws inside the pipe.

A mouse plopped onto the graystone.

My heart punched my chest and I was struck by an overwhelming urge to spring at the mouse. *No, Isla!* It was too far to reach—it would run away or jump back into the pipe. For a few beats, I didn't move, fighting to contain my excitement. Very slowly, I looked over my shoulder at Siffrin. He was hunkered low to the ground, his brush drawn up to his flank. He blinked at me. I knew what he wanted me to do: it was my turn to slimmer.

The mouse was standing a short distance from the opening to the pipe, weaving its paws through its whiskers and picking its yellow teeth. I dared not speak, even in a hushed whisper, but the chant rolled around my mind.

What was seen is unseen; what was sensed becomes senseless. What was bone is bending; what was fur is air.

I drew in my breath. Very gently, I lifted myself onto my paws, only whiskers above the ground. I stayed there, frozen, as the graystone cooled the fur of my belly. I focused on the chant, letting the words drift through me. My breath fluttered in my mouth and I swallowed it back. Keeping my body low and with steps so mindful it felt like I was barely moving, I started to edge toward the mouse. It raised its pointy face, turning a small black eye in my direction. I could sense the warmth of its skin and the staccato patter of its heart. I froze, holding back my breath while I silently repeated the chant.

What was seen is unseen; what was sensed becomes senseless.
What was bone is bending; what was fur is air.

After a moment, the mouse dropped its gaze and started to comb its oily coat.

I took another step closer. My pulse was in my tongue. My snout held firm to the scent of the mouse, my brush a weightless cloud that drifted behind me. My limbs tingled. A gauzy veil crept over my eyes: I could no longer see the mouse. There was only a twist of heat where it had once been, a shimmer against a dark horizon. I drew toward it, fastening my senses to the warmth of its body, its peppery fur. My breath, still held, beat a path over my palate.

The mouse was moving: I saw it in the eye of my thoughts. It made a stumbling leap toward me and froze. It knew that something was wrong, but it could not see me. It didn't know where to turn.

I'm doing it, Pirie—I'm doing your trick!

I wished he was here to witness this. He wouldn't believe his eyes! I was close now.

What was seen is unseen . . .

Close, but not yet. Another pawstep toward the glistening light.

What was sensed becomes senseless . . .

I pounced. With a thump of both forepaws, the mouse was down. With a bite and a jerk of my head, it was dead.

*　　*　　*

"If we keep going, we should be at the winged furless before the moon is at its highest." Siffrin was moving with quick, nervous steps, his ears rotating and flicking as he trained his attention on the deathway. The tip of his tail curled as another mangler sped alongside us.

Poised on the bank next to Siffrin, I found it hard to share his anxiety. I had slimmered—I had caught a mouse! Three others had scampered out after it, and I'd managed to trap them with Siffrin's help. My belly was full of rich, peppery meat and my thoughts were bursting with the stories I would share with my family when I reached the winged furless. Not just of the slimmering, but everything that had happened since I'd left the den. I'd tell them how I worked out the secret to avoiding manglers, that a fox was safe if she stayed on the bank. They would be amazed to hear how I'd survived alone in the Great Snarl for a whole night. And how, with Siffrin's help, I'd escaped a huge dog and fought attacking foxes.

Catching the mice had made me feel generous, and I'd gladly shared them with the red-furred fox. I watched him as he glanced along the deathway and finally crossed. As I jogged by his side, I recalled how he'd slimmered to protect me, and how he'd fought so tirelessly against Tarr and the others. Then there was the maa-sharm, when he'd shared his most precious gift—his own life source. The truth was that

Siffrin had helped a great deal . . . If he hadn't appeared when he did, I probably wouldn't be around. But I still didn't really understand him, or why he was here.

"This way." He turned along a stream of the deathway and I kept pace at his side. A bustle of furless trotted over the graystone, their hind paws clacking on the hard ground. He snorted in frustration. "They're everywhere."

The sun was still up—what did he expect? I stopped short of saying so.

"We'll have to move quickly," he went on, not waiting for me to reply before hurrying down the bank, between the legs of furless. One shrieked fearfully as we approached, stumbling out of our way. Others pointed and yipped.

What was bone is bending; what was fur is air.

Holding my breath, I slipped between them, careful not to let them bump into me. They didn't look—they didn't see me.

"Isla!" Siffrin paused up ahead. There was a disapproving wrinkle to his muzzle. "You shouldn't slimmer all the time."

I blew out my chest, panting for air. "Why not? It works against the furless!" I hopped up and down, unable to contain my excitement.

"The furless hardly see what's in front of their noses. Save slimmering for foxes or dogs, or for when you hunt— it's a waste of maa. If you keep it up, you'll be exhausted by nightfall." His eyes trailed over the crowds of furless and the spy holes of passing manglers. "What a miserable place. The stench . . ."

The soft white fur of his ears flicked in and out of view. I blinked at him. "Wouldn't it be better to walk at night?"

He cringed against the wall as a furless with huge rear paws stomped by less than a brush-length from him. "The more ground we can cover by day, the better off we'll be. You can see it in the wildways, the first signs of early bud. I need to be out of the Graylands long before malinta—I don't want to lose any time."

We stalked beside the wall, doing our best to avoid the furless. It wasn't easy, particularly since several were leaning against the wall, sitting on the bank of the deathway. It was odd to see furless on the ground. These ones looked young, although not as young as cubs, with high cheekbones and hollow eyes.

"What *is* malinta?" I asked, curiosity overcoming my fear of a rebuke. I wasn't just a fox cub now, I was a fox who slimmered. I deserved some answers.

Siffrin ran when he passed the young furless, then stopped and trained his gaze on the curving deathway. "Malinta falls twice over the full rotation of the seasons, when day and night are of equal length. It's an important time. Most cubs are born at the second malinta, when the frost eases and buds appear in the trees."

Instinctively I glanced up, but there were no trees along the deathway. It had lapsed into a wide, ugly path and dirty gray buildings. Even their spy holes were webbed in filth. One nearest to us by the bank of the deathway had shattered. Another was covered with a wooden board.

"Is that why you said I was born early?"

Siffrin glanced at me—a flash of those bronze, black-rimmed eyes. He started along the bank and I walked alongside him. "Your coat is already ginger. You must have been born in the deep chill." He frowned, his whiskers flexing forward. "I think that may be why you're different."

"Different how?" I wasn't sure I should ask. It was probably a criticism. Siffrin's steps faltered. As the deathway divided, he looked uncertain. Behind him, a large furless was shuffling along the bank, clutching a stick. My ears pressed back and I whined at the red-furred fox. "Look out . . . that furless is scowling at you."

Siffrin wheeled around. "How can you tell?"

I thought about it a moment. "I guess I've been in the Snarl long enough. Their faces change when they're angry."

Just as I'd uttered these words, the furless started barking. He raised his stick and shook it threateningly at Siffrin, who arched his back, tail low and ears flat. The furless thwacked the stick against the graystone. It wasn't close enough to Siffrin to catch him, but the motion alarmed the red-furred fox, who yelped and scrambled into me. We tumbled and leaped to our paws.

Siffrin's tail beat back and forth. "Let's get out of here!"

We darted along the bank as the angry furless yelled at us. I glanced over my shoulder. He was shaking his stick in the air as other furless clucked around him.

We turned onto the next stretch of the deathway. More furless swarmed on the bank. Siffrin sighed in exasperation. "This is impossible." He started ahead with tentative steps, but I had stopped, struggling to grasp at smells beneath the acid pall of the Snarl. He padded back to me. "What is it?"

Ash and cinder.

Was it just the stench of the deathway?

Siffrin started sniffing urgently, his snout bobbing up and down. His ears swiveled forward and he looked at me.

"I'm not sure . . ." I spoke slowly, still drinking in the foul air. "Maybe Karka's skulk."

He raised his muzzle, lips slightly parted. "Here? It's not even dark yet . . ." He surveyed the area. Everywhere we turned there were furless. His hairs rose along his back. He looked like a lost cub.

So many furless. Maybe to get away from them, you had to look at their world from another angle. My eyes climbed the crumbling redstone walls of the Snarl. Between two dens that hunkered alongside each other, I noticed a series of metal steps. Throwing my head back, I could see that they led all the way up the wall.

"How about the top of that den?"

Siffrin followed my gaze. "Good idea!" he yipped. Heat pulsed in my chest and I wagged my tail. He let me lead. I pounced up the cool steps that hung onto the redstone, my claws clattering on the metal. The world of bustle and stench seemed to fall away as I mounted. I didn't look down, fixing my attention on each step. There was a gap between the top step and the roof. I took a deep breath and flung myself over, landing on red tiles.

I turned to watch Siffrin climb the last steps and my jaw fell slack. The deathway was far below us. My belly lurched. Everything seemed strange from up here: the manglers looked smaller, no bigger than foxes—a pigeon on the edge of the roof seemed so much larger than them. Buildings jostled for space, shunting each other like mushrooms that crept up in the gloom. I could see a jumble of neighboring roofs, where more pigeons cooed and nested, safe from the dangers of the Snarl.

I peered into the distance, wondering where we'd find the winged furless. She couldn't be far away now. Hope tingled my fur as I remembered Fa's words.

Dreams are the beginning.

Siffrin climbed the tiles alongside me. His eyes widened, his tail lashing as he took in the rooftops and the deathway, shrunken in the distance.

Together, we crept to the edge of the roof. The wind flew free, without buildings to block its path. The cool air lifted my fur and played with my tail. I sank onto my belly, my eyes trained on the deathway. The furless surged along its banks, barking to one another, but their voices were lost up here on the roof. The call of the Great Snarl had faded to a dull murmur.

Siffrin settled at my side. "It's incredible . . ." He shook his head. "This was a good idea. No one would think to look for us here." His sweet, musky scent drifted toward me. "I don't seem to be able to smell danger anymore. My senses are wilting like a thirsty grass stem. I have to get back to the Wildlands."

I felt a curious tug at my chest at the thought of him leaving. Instead of looking at him, I watched two furless embrace on the bank of the deathway. Others ignored them, brushing past, as though they had slimmered and were invisible.

"There's a hint of violet in the sky. Back in the Wildlands, the air grows purple and pink as it turns to dusk." Siffrin let out a long breath. "I don't belong here."

I felt a pang of resentment as I raised my head to the sun,

which was melting beyond clouds. A faint haze hung in the gray clouds. What was so good about the Wildlands, anyway? Who needed purple skies? "I suppose Jana will be waiting for you?"

"She's probably already wondering why I haven't returned. She might need me for another mission."

My ears flicked back. "What kind of mission?"

From the corner of my eye, I saw him settle his head on his forepaws. "A fox is lost to the Elders, beyond the fur and sinew of the greatest of Canista's cubs."

I glanced at him. "What's that supposed to mean?"

Siffrin didn't look up. "I'm not sure. It's something Jana said—I probably shouldn't be telling you."

"Does she always speak in riddles?"

He tipped his head toward me, his eyes sparkling. "Occasionally," he admitted.

For a moment I was held in that bronze gaze, with its flecks of green and gold. I ran my tongue over my muzzle. "My family is lost. Do you think it could be them?"

Siffrin's voice was soft. "Jana only spoke of one fox."

"Could it be one of the Elders? The ones who didn't come to the . . . oh, the place you mentioned?"

"The Elder Rock." He turned his attention back to the deathway, down below us, and I did the same. Manglers lurched and growled as furless pressed between them in reckless clusters. "Maybe," he replied, noncommittal. "The bank of the deathway where those furless are crossing . . . we were just there. Now it seems so far away."

I wasn't paying attention. A tingle of excitement had caught me by surprise, a curious thought: what if the lost fox was Pirie? Jana seemed so keen for Siffrin to find him. What was so special about my brother? What did it mean to be lost beyond the fur and sinew of the greatest of Canista's cubs?

As the deathway faded back into focus, my gaze rested on a furless who was wrapped in a glossy red robe. She strode along the street, her robe bright against the graystone. As she stopped a moment to look about, I noticed a tiny path that led off the deathway. Gray upon gray, shadows shifted. Eyes glinted in the darkness. I craned my head and my ears pricked up. Was a group of cats down there?

The red-robed furless passed the dark path. Another furless paused in front of it, blocking my view. When he moved on, I saw the outline of several creatures, with angular snouts and pointed ears. One figure stepped out in front of the others. Her ears were rounded and her frame was thick and muscular.

We were just there.

"Karka!" I yelped, every hair on my body alert, every whisker like a trembling breath.

I could hear the gasp on Siffrin's lips. His head was close to mine as he scanned the deathway, his gaze roving to the darkened path. The whites of his eyes shone like crescent moons. He shrank from the edge of the roof, the tiles clinking beneath his paws. "Get back!" he whined. "Come away from there. You don't know what she's capable of! If Karka sees you, we're as good as dead."

13

The gathering darkness leached color from the clouds. Already, the murmur of violet was lapsing into a dreary fug. Across the Great Snarl, brightglobes flickered to life. The eyes of manglers were luminous; the deathway glittered. Beneath the flickering hum it was hard to make out details: the skeins of furless streaming over the banks . . . the shiny manglers and their long, hard snouts . . .

The shapes of foxes as they crouched in the shadows.

Siffrin prowled over the roof and I crept behind him, low to the tiles with my paws splayed wide to keep my balance. His ears rotated. "Stay back from the edge."

The tiles rose to a peak over the middle of the building. We scrambled toward it, half bounding, half crawling. I didn't want to think of how far up we were, or the twinkling deathway down below. We risked a look across the Snarl.

The buildings surrounding us stooped in an ugly jumble. Peaked rooftops ruptured the skyline as far as the eye could see. There was nothing glossy or slick about them, not like the towering structures I'd spied from the beast dens.

Clouds sprawled and eddied. The shimmering buildings must be swallowed within them, there but invisible, like a slimmering fox.

Siffrin rose up on his paws, peering toward the deathway. I tried my best to do the same, but I couldn't see the ground from this angle on the roof.

"Is it Karka?" What if I'd gotten it wrong?

Siffrin's voice was thin. "It's her. She's with six more foxes. I can't make out Tarr . . . He's probably with the rest of the skulk."

My ears flicked back. So many of them. "Are you sure they can't see you?"

"They won't think to look up." Even so, he sank lower behind the peak of the roof.

"How do you know that's not the whole skulk?"

Siffrin spoke absently, his attention fixed on the deathway. "There were twelve in all, weren't there?"

This reminded me of something he had said a few days ago. *I must have seen a dozen foxes in her skulk . . .*

It hadn't struck me at the time, but now I paused, craning my neck, trying to see over the roof. I pushed up on my forelegs. I could just make out the far bank. I scanned the graystone for Karka. It was much harder to see with the brightglobes blazing beneath us.

Dread bit my throat.

A group of foxes had gathered at the shaded entrance to a furless den—a mass of narrow limbs and flicking tails. At the front, I made out Karka's lumbering frame. There was something lumpy around her shoulders, as though the fur was bunching.

For an instant, I was crouching outside my den, pressed against the ivy that hung off the fence. The den was half-hidden beyond the copse amid a lattice of fallen branches. It was hard to see what was going on in there. I could just make out the shapes of unfamiliar foxes, maybe five or six, creeping about, digging and yelping to each other. They were met by a thickset vixen . . .

Back on the roof, overlooking the Snarl, a skittering chill ran down my back. "There weren't that many."

"What's that?" Siffrin was hardly listening to me. His ears were flat and his eyes were round and fearful. "We'll be all right if we hide up here. Let's get behind the middle of the roof. That would be safer. The wind is high, I don't think our scents will reach them." He hooked a forepaw around the peak of the roof and started to lift himself over. "Come on, Isla."

I stayed where I was. "There weren't that many," I repeated.

He slipped over the peak without a sound, his movement liquid, like a cat. "You can't see them from there, you're too small. You don't know how many there are." He was already edging down the tiles on the far side of the peak, his brush billowing in the wind. He turned to me, ears pricked. "Aren't you coming? We should be . . ." His words dissolved. "What's wrong?"

A slither of acid snagged in my throat.

What made Siffrin so sure there were twelve in the skulk? If he had followed me from the wildway to my den—watched Karka's skulk emerge amid swirling smoke—he could only have seen six or seven, as I had.

Darklands fox. Deceitful fox.

I swallowed hard. "Have you met Karka before? Do you know . . . her skulk?"

His muzzle tensed. "What do you mean?"

"Just that. Do you know them? The way that Tarr seemed to know you?"

His ears swiveled forward. "Of course not. What Tarr said was a mistake. I've already told you . . . Isla, what's going on?" He dropped his gaze, glancing over the deathway and back to me, but his eyes did not meet mine. "We shouldn't be standing here, at the top of the roof. If they look up . . ."

"But you knew about their eyes." I remembered what

he'd said after the skulk attacked. *The gray-faced one—did you look into his eyes? Were they red?*

"Jana warned me to look out for them."

It wasn't just Tarr. I thought of his gasp as he'd stooped at my side moments ago when he'd spotted Karka. The whites of his eyes were like crescent moons. Even on the deathway, with Tarr upon him, he'd never seemed so afraid.

You don't know what she's capable of!

But what if Siffrin did know? What if he'd seen her kill?

My body was rigid—my voice was ice. "You're lying."

Fear tightened at his muzzle. His fur was beat back by the gusts that leaped over the rooftop.

I bared my teeth. "Who are they to you?"

"Nothing, I promise. You've got it wrong." He appealed with his eyes, bronze flecked with dancing flames. He reached out a forepaw, which quivered in the wind.

"Get away!" I snapped at his paw, and he flinched.

The color of his eyes was scorched on my mind, red flecks spinning, making me dizzy.

He threw down his forepaws, bowing in a conciliatory gesture, his head cocked, panting like a cub. "Come on," he whimpered. "I may not have told you everything—Jana forbade it—but it's not what you think. I'm on your side."

He looked so sincere. Could I be wrong? I thought of how he'd fought to protect me; I remembered the maa he had shared with me. But still I hovered before the peak of the roof. The sky around Siffrin hummed in gray, and he alone was a flash of color, brilliant red against the darkness. He shuffled his paws in playful submission, ears bending sideways, head slightly cocked.

There was a splitting crack as the tiles broke beneath him.

Before my eyes, he started to skid.

"Siffrin!" I shrieked as he pitched backward, tumbling down the slanted roof. I took the peak in a single bound. There was a flash of red fur as he skated with the falling tiles, a throttled whimper on his tongue. At the edge of the roof, a plunging drop, a glimpse of the graystone far below. A premonition of shattering bones, my heart in my throat, my brush taut with horror.

"Hold on!" I yelped as I skidded down toward him, my paws reckless on the clanking tiles. Siffrin clutched wildly to the edge of the roof, his hind legs dangling high over the graystone. I slid on my belly as fast as I dared. Bracing, I came to a halt by his straining forelegs.

He shook with effort. "I can't get up . . ." A tile came loose beneath him. He slipped back a whisker-length as it lurched under his grip. He gritted his teeth as the tile came free, careening down to the graystone path.

It shattered into tiny pieces.

I crouched by his neck and closed my teeth around his scruff. I tugged and yanked with all my might, but he was

168

too heavy for me to lift. My eyes were clamped shut as I strained with effort, but I felt him slipping away from me, creeping toward the fall.

I released the fur at his neck and my eyes locked on his. They were wild and round. I felt a stab of heat as he held my gaze. The gray sky faded in a twist of gold as Siffrin's eyes glowed orange and shimmering green. A shudder of energy passed between us. A flash of white light.

Siffrin was struggling, his muzzle clenched but his eyes still round. With a grunt, he was back on the roof, his hind paws gathered beneath his belly, wheezing and grasping great gulps of air. I buried my head against his shoulder, my body quaking with relief. He hadn't fallen—he was here, by my side.

Blearily, I raised my head. A speckle of rain wetted my nose. Dark clouds scudded overhead. When would the first drop fall on the deathway? I squinted through the hum of the brightglobes.

The rush of dark bodies.

Heads raised in threat.

A shot of white terror. "It's Karka—she's seen us."

His head snapped up. "Where are they now?"

I squinted through the fizz of the brightglobes. I had lost Karka's skulk in the flurry of furless. Over and over I combed the deathway, but I couldn't unpick them from the rumbling manglers.

"Maybe I'm wrong," I said at last. "I can't see them anymore."

A frightful snicker exploded above us. At the peak of the roof, where some tiles were missing, three narrow faces broke out against the clouds.

Siffrin rose onto his shaking paws. "We have to run!"

"Careful," I begged him. He was so close to the edge of the roof. With a grimace I remembered the shattered tile.

The foxes were stalking over the peak, edging toward us with teeth exposed. Now there were four . . . then there were five. Each bore the mark of the broken rose, barely visible in the low light. Karka had not yet materialized—was she down in the deathway, or creeping behind them?

Siffrin swallowed. "We'll have to jump."

I followed his gaze to the next building. Its brown roof was a few brush-lengths lower than us, but before it there was a sizable gap, easily the length of a full-grown fox, where the two walls parted and the tile had slipped and smashed against the graystone.

"I can't," I whined. "It's too far to jump."

He gave my nose a gentle lick. "I know you can do it—I've felt your maa. How do you think I had the strength to climb back onto the roof?"

A shudder of energy passed between us. A flash of white light.

"Was that maa-sharm?" I gasped in amazement.

Siffrin nudged my muzzle. "You did it without even thinking." He glanced at the gap. "Your maa is strong. You can do anything—better to try than to wait for them."

The clatter of claws from the foxes behind us.

Siffrin's face was anxious. "We will go together. Are you ready to jump?"

My heart beat so hard that it felt like my chest was bursting. The foxes were pawsteps away from us. Already, Siffrin was back on his haunches. "Wait!" I yelped as he took a deep breath.

"Isla!" he barked, and my legs started tensing. "Now!"

I felt myself springing through the air. In an instant, I was soaring—forepaws diving over the roof. The wind clasped at my belly as I flew over the path. A moment of free fall; a flash of graystone; and *smack!* my forepaws hit the next roof, my back legs thumping on the brown tiles. There was thunder inside my ears, a shrill of excitement that nearly overwhelmed me.

Siffrin's eyes were glowing as he turned just ahead of me. "You did it!" he yelped, with a *wow-wow-wow!*

I clambered to his side and he licked my nose. "Are we safe?" I breathed.

"Not yet," he murmured. I spun around to see five foxes approaching, lined up at the edge of the other building. Their eyes were black and ringed in red.

Poised by my side, Siffrin started to chant.

"I am the fur that ruffles your back. I am the twist and shake of your tail . . ."

His slim legs thickened, his long ears shrank: I watched him transform into a huge black dog—the one from the yard with the bubbling jowls. He dropped his head and growled so loudly that I flinched, even though I knew it was Siffrin.

The foxes on the neighboring roof cowered at the sight of the dog, backing up along the tiles.

A rumble came from behind them and their ears dropped. The looming figure of a thickset fox pressed up on the peak of the roof with her forepaws. Unlike the others, there was no rose-shaped scar on her foreleg.

Karka.

She glared at Siffrin with her roving gray eye. "Get them!" she shrieked at her skulk. "You pathetic cowards! Don't you realize it's just a fox in disguise?"

At her command, they rolled back on their haunches, preparing to attack.

Siffrin was hurrying away, shifting back into his own form. "It's no use. We'll have to keep going." We scrambled up to the peak of the brown-tiled roof.

"Can't you change into a cat?" I was thinking quickly, remembering how felines could slink and pounce, so much lighter on their paws.

His ears flipped back. "No," he told me. "Wa'akkir is governed by strict codes of foxlore. It only works for cubs of Canista."

He'd said that before, but I must have forgotten. I turned to see the foxes leaping, landing on the brown tiles behind us. They started edging over the rooftop as we skirted down the other side of the roof.

The next roof was flat and less than a brush-length away. We leaped it quickly as the foxes gathered pace. Dark clouds tumbled on the blustering wind. The edges of the skyline receded as the smattering of rain turned into a shower.

"This way," said Siffrin, dashing across the flat roof. He pounced onto another, built of hard gray tiles. I sprang behind him. My fur was alive as I swooped through the air, my paw pads skidding on the shiny rooftop. My claws scraped against tiles as I fought for balance.

Karka's skulk was gaining on us, fluid against the damp sky. Their bodies seemed to melt into rainfall, slipping in and out of view.

Over the tiles, across the peaked rooftop, Siffrin stumbled to a halt with a cry. I followed his gaze to the edge, looked beyond it with a shudder of fright. The next roof was slick with black tiles. The gap between the buildings was further this time—right above a path of the deathway, at least several brush-lengths wide. Long depths below us, a mangler rumbled through, its bright eyes blazing yet blind to our presence.

Siffrin's whiskers trembled. "We'll fall to our deaths."

"How fitting," screeched Karka. "Your bones will be food for rats!" She was climbing over the shiny gray tiles. Her skulk fell into step at her flanks, a wall of foxes closing in on us.

"What if we run at it?" I found myself whispering.

Already the foxes were brush-lengths away. I could make out the details of their rain-slicked heads. This close, I saw that in place of Karka's missing eye, there was a throbbing knot of purple flesh. Her haunches dropped and she snapped her teeth, so close to my tail that the white hairs fluttered. Fear gave me courage and I found myself running. I cleared the sloping roof with great, gulping bounds.

A moment later I was flying.

Rain dazzled my eyes and the wind stroked my fur. The lashing downpour blinded my vision. My pounce was spinning into a tumble. I reached out my forepaws, but felt only air. A claw of panic ripped through my body. Then *thump!* I slammed against the neighboring rooftop. My eyes flicked open—I was safe!

Thump!

Siffrin was by my side. We hopped and whooped, soaked to the skin.

"We're alive!" I yipped, too excited to breathe.

"Get them!" shrieked Karka, but the other foxes faltered. "Get them or I'll tear out your filthy throats!"

I backed along the wet black tiles, up to the safety of the ridged peak. Siffrin huddled next to me. We blinked through the rain at the far roof, where the foxes were balancing along the gray tiles. From here, the gap between the buildings seemed even wider, yawning over the path in the deathway. My body quivered with excitement and terror, astonished that we had jumped across.

"I'll go, Karka," barked a tawny vixen. I had seen her before—she was one of the foxes who had circled my family's den. She lurched over the tiles of the neighboring rooftop, her lips pulled back in a petrified grin. She gave a small cry as she vaulted over the edge. Under driving rain, her body extended, forepaws paddling as she swept through the air. She started to tip, her brush flipping upward. Short of the rooftop, she plummeted down.

Siffrin buried his head against my shoulder, but I did not turn. My eyes were fixed on the vixen. I watched as her claws swept the edge of the rooftop—as she dropped, headfirst, to the deathway below. From where we were perched, I couldn't see the impact, and the rain distorted the cracking limbs. I was spared the mangle of her broken body.

Her death reached me only as an echo: from the round dark eyes of the foxes lined up on the opposite roof. Each head dipped—drenched and fearful—reflecting the horror they saw below.

Siffrin's muzzle was lost in my fur, the faintest whimper against the rain.

Only Karka stared beyond the deathway, at the roof where I stood at Siffrin's side. Through the downpour she lifted her snout in challenge. Her gaze was unflinching. Unrepentant.

14

The wind wailed as it picked up speed. It seemed to shake Siffrin from his despair as he raised his head and peered across the rooftops.

He had to bark to be heard above the deluge. "I don't think the Taken can reach us. Slowly, it's slippery. One wrong move . . ." he didn't finish. He didn't have to—we both knew what one wrong move would mean.

I stalked behind him, my belly grazing the tiles. My sodden fur was weighing me down. Rivulets tumbled between my paws, enticing me back along the slope of the roof. I gritted my teeth, resisting the pull. When I reached the peak where Siffrin was waiting, I paused to look over my shoulder. Mist swirled around us, hugging the skyline. Through sheets of rain I saw the hunching shape of Karka's skulk, poised on the edge of the neighboring rooftop, across the path of the deathway. Their contours bled into the downpour, like ghostly apparitions. I squinted, trying to untangle them from the mist, but instead they faded beneath its white pelt.

"This side is better," Siffrin barked.

I hooked my forelegs onto the peak, but my limbs shuddered with fatigue. As I tried to haul myself over I felt my back paws slide. I took a deep breath and tried again, clinging to the tiles as the rain lashed my face. It was hopeless. I shut my eyes and pictured the tawny vixen as she hurtled over the rooftop to the deathway. The grin of terror on her face.

Teeth closed gently around my scruff and I felt a powerful tug as Siffrin lifted me clear of the peak. He set me down on the other side. No one had carried me like that since I was a young cub.

Dimly I remembered Ma scooping me up and delivering me back to the den. "You shouldn't venture so far alone," she'd scolded. "I looked for you and you'd disappeared." Her voice had grown soft as she'd licked my muzzle. "A fox should be cautious. You're so bold, Isla, too fearless for this world." I remembered the sweet warmth of her fur and the tickle of her whiskers as they brushed against mine.

Who's disappeared now? I asked the clouds, and the rain, and the mist that clung to the rooftops. A ma wasn't supposed to abandon her cub. The seed of a black thought took root inside me—could it be that my family didn't want to be found?

I shook the droplets of rain from my eyes. Siffrin was standing over me. Soaked to his skin, his frame seemed slighter, his shoulders stooped, bedraggled and slender. The murk of the night had sapped the red from his fur. The rain had depleted his bushy coat, diminishing him to an ordinary creature. Only his black-rimmed eyes were the same—large and haunted, touched with light.

A jumble of questions still tussled inside me. Who was Karka and how did Siffrin know her? Who was the Master, and who were the Taken? Siffrin claimed he'd never met the ghoulish skulk with the rose-shaped scars, that if Tarr thought he recognized him, he was mistaken. The red-furred fox had risked so much to help me, but deep in my belly I knew he was lying.

Siffrin blinked and gave a shake, releasing me from my muddled thoughts.

"The next roof meets this one. I think there may be a way down." He turned away from me, staring through the mist. "Are you all right across the last of the tiles?"

I gave a small yip to show that I was. He started easing himself along the roof, forepaws splayed as he slid with the gushing rain. I could just see a wall at the bottom, another flat roof without a gap. Siffrin stepped down onto the roof and waited for me to join him. Together, we hurried over the building, treading deep puddles that sloshed at our paws.

The next roof was close and a good pounce lower.

"We're getting there," Siffrin barked over the rain.

No more, I thought unhappily. But it looked like a clear jump, and easy enough if we kept our balance. "Let's get it over with!"

He cocked his head. "We'll do it together."

We sprang from the flat roof through driving rain. It felt like falling through a blizzard. We landed on tiles very close to each other with a *slosh!* and a *smash!*

The roof started quaking.

"What is it?" I yipped, my claws scrambling on tiles. I couldn't get a foothold and I floundered, tail spinning.

"The ground's giving way!" Siffrin barked in alarm.

The building sighed and started shaking. There was a loud creak as I tripped onto my flank. And a splintering crack as we plunged into darkness.

Billows of white dust toppled down on me. I couldn't see Siffrin, but I could hear him coughing. My heart hammered so hard that I was only vaguely aware of the other sounds crashing around me, of shattering wood and splitting stone. The dust was everywhere, in my eyes, in my throat. I lapped at the air and tasted it, powdery and metallic.

I was hunched on top of a mound of boards. Had they come from the roof? Tentatively, I reached out a paw. The boards trembled and I froze.

"Siffrin, are you hurt?"

He coughed again and cleared his throat. "I'm fine."

"We fell through the roof!" There was a deep groan overhead and a shower of dust so thick I could feel it settling on my fur. I gave myself a shake and heard a threatening growl from the boards below. I blinked upward and caught a lash of rain across my brow. "I think the roof may be collapsing. It seems to be getting worse."

I scrambled over the shifting boards, trying to find solid ground. Instead I stumbled into Siffrin's wet flank. I gave a little cry, my heart lurching against my ribs.

"It's all right," he soothed. "I can see a way out."

I didn't know how he could see anything through the twirling dust, but I grew calmer, drawing in shallow breaths so as not to gulp the dirty air.

Siffrin started to move. "Stay close." He climbed down the boards and I huddled by his side, feeling the muscles flex beneath his sodden coat. I reached out a forepaw and touched solid ground. With relief, I sprang down next to Siffrin onto the floor. As the dust began to settle, I could see the outline of an open doorway. A rip overhead, another shower of dust, and Siffrin and I were flying out of the exit further into the building.

A furless was barking close by. I could hear the floor squeak as he charged toward us. We scrambled past him to a set of steps as he wailed, his forepaws clutching his head. As Siffrin bolted down the steps, I paused to watch the furless. He stood perfectly still, paws fixed to his head, as mist and rain spun down from the hole in the roof.

"I think we're in a furless den!" I barked as I hopped down the steps. Dust still masked my senses, but the smell of furless was pungent. I took in the spongy beige floor, where I spotted a trail of Siffrin's dusty paw prints. Through a doorway to the side, I saw a large chamber with images of furless all over the walls, their even white teeth flashing ominously. I scanned the large brown objects piled on the ground, where I guessed they rested. Most of the walls in the den were pale yellow, but straight ahead of us one was ridged and white.

Soaking wet and covered with dust, Siffrin was a ghostly shadow of himself. I wouldn't have recognized him had we passed on the deathway. He trod nervously over the beige floor. "We have to get out of here. We shouldn't be this close to the furless. Jana said *never* to approach them." His tail jerked with agitation.

"There'll be a way out." I remembered the den that looked out over our patch. The furless built exits on each side. We just had to find one . . .

There was the sound of jangling metal. A moment later,

the white stretch of wall swung open and a furless appeared, soaked to the skin. It was a door! The furless stared at us, her jaw falling slack. Beyond her I saw the deathway, where the rain still dropped in sheets.

My voice was a low growl. "We have to get out—before the door closes."

"Jana said—"

"Come on!" I cried, and I scurried passed the legs of the furless. She stumbled back with a squeal and stood there, gaping. But Siffrin hadn't followed me—he crouched in the den, reluctant to approach the furless. "Hurry up!" I called. "She's not going to hurt you!"

He made a quick move and the furless yelped. Siffrin shrank back, his tail-tip jerking, his ears shifting to the sides of his head at sharp angles.

"Siffrin!" I whined.

His eyes were on me as he hovered uncertainly. He took a deep breath and burst through the doorway. His flank smacked the furless near the base of her leg, but he was out. There was a loud bang as the door slammed shut behind us. Spooked, we charged along the graystone. Streaks of dust ran into my eyes as rain tumbled over us, battering the deathway.

No one was chasing us—still, we kept running. Karka's skulk must have slunk into some dark pathway. Brisk looks over our shoulders confirmed the bank was deserted. The furless had fled inside their dens. Only manglers still prowled, with their white eyes weeping.

Siffrin held back so we could run side by side, turning sharp bends on the bank of the deathway, along redstone buildings and under an arch. When we reached a wildway, he finally slowed down, jogging to a stop as I gulped for air.

"How are you doing?" he shouted over the rain. The droplets clung and pattered off his whiskers.

"Fine," I barked back, though now that the exhilaration of our escape was fading, I could feel an ache expanding through my paws.

He cocked his head. "I never thought I'd be so pleased to walk on graystone." He lifted his muzzle to the pounding rain. It had cleansed the coating of dust from his fur. I followed his gaze and my belly tensed—from the ground, the roofs seemed impossibly high. They lapsed into mist, lost in banks of cloud.

Siffrin dipped his head to scan the deathway. "At least the rain will wash away our scents. No one could track us in this weather."

I turned between the brightglobes. Where had we come from? I'd completely lost my bearings.

Siffrin took a step closer to me. A blue tint shone in the blacks of his eyes. He seemed to hesitate, whiskers fluttering in the wind. "Do you have the strength to go a little further? Or would you rather . . . Do you want to rest?"

Weariness was taking hold, but his question intrigued me. "What is it?"

He ran his tongue over the white of his muzzle before turning to trot through the rain. I followed him between the railings of the wildway, over short-shorn grass and verges turning muddy. I blinked through the downpour, wondering where he was taking me. We slunk through another set of railings, but there was no sign of the deathway. On the far side of the wildway was a row of tall furless dens. In front of them was a huge stone yard.

Siffrin stopped at the edge of the wildway. He caught my eye with a wary look. I gazed beyond him, over the courtyard. There was a large object at the center. At first it looked like a giant furless—a female with arching wings . . . My legs were moving with a will of their own. At the base of my ears, my pulse was thrumming. There was the furless with the cool stone body, her robe rigid against the wind, her wings raised, preparing for flight. She towered above me, hard and fearless, slick with rain.

Excitement surged through me.

I approached the great furless without any fear. I knew she wasn't real—she was made of rock. A skip of my heart as I sniffed her paws; I thought I detected a flicker of Pirie. That was enough to make me yip with elation, to send my brush into furious wagging.

Calm down, Isla, I berated myself. Carefully, I sniffed

again. If only the sky would take back its rain. In its cold damp sting, scents diminished to air.

The wind was baying as I raised my muzzle, scanning the courtyard for signs of my family. Had Ma passed here, her brush drifting behind her? Was Fa close by, sitting, waiting for me?

I turned around slowly.

There was no one there.

No foxes, no furless: not even a pigeon. Only Siffrin stood in the distance, a silhouette against the rain. My glimmer of hope was dwindling to darkness. A faint scent of Pirie wasn't enough. He had been here, but he'd left for who-knew-where . . . There was no hint that he was with Ma, Fa, or Greatma—not even a sign that he was still alive. A sharp sense of dread clutched at my belly. It had been there for days, though I'd tried to ignore it.

I'd looked so hard and had come so far, but the rain had washed away the clues. It swept over me and my weary legs buckled, my whine carried off by the howling wind.

15

I shuffled numbly to Siffrin's side, padding over the graystone courtyard. We wandered down a narrow passage, retracing a path to the deathway. Rain still hammered onto the graystone, splashing back in a fine white mist. I hardly noticed its icy touch, or Siffrin's muzzle at my shoulder as he nudged me along.

"A little further, we'll rest soon."

I no longer cared where he was leading me. I had lost all sense of my family's presence, had seen the winged furless and discovered nothing. Disappointment weighed thickly on my sodden coat, and beyond it there was something more frightening, a clawing dread I had pushed away for days.

My eyes strayed over the graystone. Water streamed along the edges of the bank, sweeping up leaves and the debris the furless scattered wherever they went. There was nothing familiar about this stretch of the deathway, and yet it looked like every other part of the Great Snarl—colorless, characterless, and gray. Disoriented, I raised my snout. I couldn't even see the beast dens on the pinnacle over the Snarl, beyond the murky horizon.

"We need to get out of this rain," Siffrin murmured.

Along the edge of the bank he found an alleyway too narrow for manglers to enter. Redstone walls rose on either side, coming together in an arch. Siffrin paused at the entrance, sniffing. He slipped into the alleyway toward a couple of huge bins and turned to me with a doubtful look. "It won't be the most comfortable place to rest, but at least it's dry."

My ears flicked back and I slid beneath the bins. There wasn't much room to move. The smell of rank meat engulfed my nose. I sighed and lowered my head onto my paws as Siffrin eased himself next to me.

He blinked at me with concern. "You're shivering."

"Am I?" My body rippled with small shudders. I hadn't even noticed.

Siffrin huddled close and drew his long brush around me. The musky scent of his wet coat drowned out the odor of the bins. Cold and bewildered, I leaned against him, comforted by the heat of his body. I hadn't curled up with anyone since my family had disappeared. I felt as though I was drifting—that I was tumbling closer to a steep drop, one that beckoned me darkly—and only Siffrin's warmth kept holding me back.

The rain must have eased a little. I could hear it drumming against the graystone outside the domed alley-way as exhaustion took hold and I drifted to sleep.

Tap-tap-tap.

Tap-tap-tap.

Rain pattered the leafless branches of the trees, slipping onto the long grass of the wildway. Pirie was crunching down on a small yellow flower, his muzzle wrinkling.

"Why are you eating that if it's so disgusting?" I skipped toward him and batted at his whiskers, but he twisted away from me and kept chewing.

"It's a superpetal," he rasped, swallowing it down with a grimace. "It's going to make me grow strong and wise."

I trilled in amusement. "Did Greatma tell you that?"

He raised his muzzle proudly. "I don't need to be *told*. You can see from the color, it's got to be healthy."

I bit off a petal and spat it out. "Yuck! It's bitter." I shook my fur. Rain was creeping down my hairs, cooling my skin. I circled Pirie, swatting his tail.

He took on an authoritative voice. "Bright colors mean things are good for you, little fox."

I gave my fur a rough shake. As though *he* knew any-thing! I thought of all the tastiest things, and how they were brown or gray: mice, voles, pigeons . . . I was about to argue when I heard Fa. "Pirie? Isla? Where are you?"

We trilled back and he jogged through the grass toward us. His white bib was glossy in the rain. He shook his ears and touched our noses. "Greatma wants you inside until the rain clears."

I glanced up at the clouds, foreseeing hours trapped in the den. "But it isn't heavy!"

"It's heavy enough."

My ears flipped back. "*You* stay out in the rain, Fa."

"It's different for me," he said mildly. "Adult foxes have thicker coats." His glance strayed to Pirie. "What are you eating, cubling?"

"I'm going to be big like you!" Pirie yipped, tearing off another yellow flower. "Then I can stay out all the time, even in storms."

Fa nipped him on the ear. "You will be, but not by eating petals. We'll find you both a couple of plump rats."

Pirie spat out the flower and hopped on the spot. "Isla doesn't need a whole rat!" he protested with a wicked glint in his eye. "She's too small. I can help her with it."

"It's *because* I'm small that I deserve more than you." I nipped him gently on the back leg. "I need the rats much more than you do. Isn't that right, Fa? Pirie can stick to eating flowers. So much more colorful."

Fa nuzzled my ear but didn't reply as he started retracing his path through the wildway. We followed eagerly, prancing and chasing each other's tails. Ma and Greatma were hovering on the fallen branch that led to our patch. The rain streaked their fur and darkened their faces. As Fa leaped onto the branch, the sky grew gloomy. A deep blue swathed the horizon, crested in gray clouds. In the air's damp breath, Ma's outline shimmered. Greatma's mottled coat was silver and gold. I came to a halt, eyes widening as Pirie scampered wide loops around me.

"I heard the creature!" he yipped excitedly. "The one with the beautiful voice. It's coming from up there—let's follow it, Isla!"

Fa was easing himself along the fallen branch, his long brush swinging from side to side as he balanced next to Ma and Greatma.

He looked over his shoulder. "Isla! Pirie! You're too young to stay out in bad weather. Come inside, where it's safe and warm. Those juicy rats are waiting."

I sniffed, my tail dropping. In the fading light, the three foxes on the branch looked blurry at the edges, like buildings wrapped in mist. Only the tips of their fur stood out, twinkling like frost.

Fa's mouth moved again, but his voice melded into the rain. Soundlessly, he called to us.

Isla! Pirie!

Pirie was already far from me, running through the wild-way, into the Great Snarl. I stood fixed to the spot as drops tumbled onto my fur. Ma, Fa, and Greatma . . . their figures were dissolving. I watched them pale against the velvet of the sky. The rain washed away everything—even the brilliance of their amber eyes.

Tap-tap-tap.

The patter of time slipping forward, of memories rushing out of reach. Of the moon withdrawing in the misty sky and the sun's first, tentative glimmer.

"I didn't expect any of this." Siffrin's voice floated above me, his brush still wrapped around my flank. I kept my eyes shut, though I was waking. I felt the softness of his fur. "I thought I'd come to the Graylands, find Pirie, and leave. That's what Jana told me, to bring him to her. I didn't know he was so young. I hadn't realized that he had a family. It never occurred to me that he was a cub. Most cubs are born later . . ."

My breath jittered at the back of my throat. My whiskers tingled. "Malinta," I whispered, testing the word on my tongue. "You said they were born at malinta . . ." I kept my eyes shut, reaching through the maze of my memories. Only Pirie's face remained bright. My brother, born moments earlier than me, before the trees were in bud.

"Around malinta, yes," agreed Siffrin. "When day and

night are of equal length and Canista's Lights shine bright. A time of energy and maa—that is when most foxlings join our world."

I was only half listening, trying to remember Pirie as a young cub. In our earliest days we lay side by side, blind and helpless. I longed to return to that time, when warmth and safety was all I had ever known. "Is there something wrong with me and Pirie that we were born when the nights are long?"

Siffrin's voice was soothing. "Not *wrong* . . . You are different, Isla. I sensed that when I touched your maa. I can't stop thinking about it . . . I'd been a fool not to see it before."

My ears pricked up. "Different how?"

He paused a long while and I started to wonder if he'd fallen asleep. When he spoke, his voice was soft. I could hardly hear him over the rain on the deathway. "Your maa was dazzling . . . Beneath the light, I brushed against something fierce and powerful, like . . . like the water that thunders along the Raging River. There is strength within you, Isla."

I didn't know how to reply. My nose quivered. "But I am small, and the world is so large. You could track the deathway from dusk till dawn for days and never reach the end." I remembered the tawny vixen who had tumbled from the roof. Was her body still broken on the graystone? I felt myself reeling toward a great fall. Truths I could scarcely bear to admit gnawed at my belly. Still, I held back, fighting my instincts, unable to confront them.

Siffrin pressed closer to me, like he was scared I would slip from his grasp—as though he knew I was about to leap. "The deathway runs even further than that," he whispered. "Who knows if it ever ends?"

I wasn't listening anymore.

I was remembering things he had said to me.

I tracked you as you returned to your den and that skulk of foxes appeared . . . But what if he hadn't done that?

I thought again of his fear when he'd spotted Karka from the roof. The whites of his eyes like crescent moons.

You don't know what she's capable of!

My body had grown rigid but I didn't move, coiled tight beneath the bin. My eyes were still shut and my belly felt hard, like it was made of rock.

I spoke with a soft growl. "What did you see at my den?"

I could feel him tense next to me. "Isla . . ."

"What did Karka do, as you stood and watched?"

Siffrin's brush fell. I could sense the murmur of his pulse through his fur. "It wasn't like that. There was nothing I could do . . ."

My eyes flicked open. I could see the fall now, the lurching drop. I'd been stifling my instincts, holding on in the hope I'd gotten it wrong. But Greatma's warning wrung in my ears.

Trust no one but family, for a fox has no friends.

I slid under the bin and turned to glare at him. I knew the truth already, had suspected it when I first realized their faces were fading from my memory. But I was going to make him say it.

His bronze eyes were wide in appeal, his ears flat against his damp fur. "They were all there, the whole skulk."

"Twelve foxes," I spat.

He flinched, lowering his gaze. "Karka was furious. She cursed the will of the urban fox that would not be tamed. She had tried to take control of them . . . to force them into slavery, like the rest of her skulk. Those foxes are not there because they want to be . . ." His voice trailed off.

My lip twitched and a rumble escaped my throat. "They are the Taken."

He raised his muzzle and looked at me. "Their will has been stolen by their master, the Mage. Karka is also his servant, but unlike Tarr and the others, she does his bidding freely."

"Is that why she doesn't have that pattern on her leg? The mark like a rose?"

Siffrin swallowed. "She is not one of the Taken. She is of the Mage's Darklands skulk, an expert in foxcraft, a trained killer. Jana warned me about her, but I had no idea what she was *really* like—not until I saw it with my own eyes."

A slither of acid rose in my throat. "You watched her kill my family."

"When I arrived, it was almost over. Your ma and fa, they were already dead . . ."

Inwardly I doubled with pain, but my body stayed frozen. Siffrin started rushing his words, his voice rising as I glowered. "Your greatma was courageous. She wouldn't let Karka steal her will. She fought hard—she seemed to know some foxcraft. You should be proud of her, Isla. She was brave." He started to move toward me, but something in my face made him retreat.

"You let Karka kill them!" I cried, heat coursing through my limbs.

"I couldn't save them. Even your greatma, they had her surrounded. There were twelve of them. There was no hope."

"You could have tried! Better to have died with her than to have run away a coward."

Siffrin's muzzle was trembling as he spoke. "I was told to leave with Pirie. Jana said it was important. I didn't imagine—"

"Where is he?" I hissed. "Where is my brother?"

"He wasn't there . . . I didn't know what to do. The old fox was falling, was already wounded. They dragged her away with your ma and fa and set cinders to your den. Then I saw you arrive. I saw you run and I started to follow."

The rage was fizzing inside me now, a white, electric heat. "You let me believe they were alive!" I howled.

"I didn't know how—"

"You *liar*!" I was backing away from him, under the archway, and he was shuffling out from beneath the bin. A low light hung on the morning mist, though it was scarcely brighter than nighttime.

"Isla, if I could have saved them . . . Karka would never have let them go. And the size of her skulk, with so many Taken . . ." He gave his head a violent shake. "You don't understand what it means to have your will ripped away from you. There is no greater cruelty a fox can endure."

So much sympathy with Tarr and his kind. So much understanding for those who had killed my family. My paws quivered and my tail flew out behind me as my doubts clamored in panicked wails.

He had known Karka's name; Tarr had recognized him . . .

Darklands fox, deceitful fox . . . We have seen the mark.

My heart lurched against my chest and my eyes shot to the top of his foreleg, to the dark grooves like scorch marks outlined in the dim light.

Don't pretend you're any different from us.

Fear channeled its way beneath my fur as I realized what I'd missed all along. Concealed beneath Siffrin's vibrant red coat, hidden in plain sight, the dark red grooves had looked like nothing. But now, with his pelt clinging wetly to his skin, I saw what the curls and curves of the faded mark added up to.

A rose-shaped scar.

The same scar carved onto all of the Taken.

I stumbled back, out into the deathway. "You didn't just come across Karka's skulk at my den. You were one of them." The words sounded incredible, even to my own ears.

Siffrin stood still, his whiskers trembling. His amber eyes were etched in sorrow. *In guilt.* "Of course I wasn't."

"I don't understand." My whole body was shaking. "I thought you were helping me, guiding me from Karka's foxes. Who are the Elders? What do they want from me? *What do they want from Pirie?*"

Siffrin stalked after me but kept his distance. "It isn't how it looks."

"Really? So how is it?" Was I swaying? It felt like the ground was suddenly uneven.

"You're exhausted. You should rest."

He made a move toward me but I charged at him, rage extinguishing my fear. I pressed my muzzle to his throat. "Who *are* you really?" My lips peeled back with hatred. "Who is the Mage?"

"Calm down, Isla! You're acting crazy." Siffrin backed away. "No one knows much about him. He built his den in the Deep Forest, hidden among ancient trees. They say he bends foxcraft to his command. The skulks from the Marshlands spoke of strange noises from the forest, odd smells and disappearances . . ."

"Why did he send foxes to my skulk? Is Pirie with him?" Siffrin's hackles were rising. "Will you *calm down*?"

"Answer me!" I barked.

"I don't know what the Mage wants! But I'd guess . . . I'd guess it's something to do with Pirie's maa. If it's anything like yours."

He had looked inside me during maa-sharm. Had he seen my thoughts, just as I'd glimpsed his? Was that also part of the plan—part of his trick to find Pirie?

"And Tarr? He'd obviously seen you before."

"He could have been from a Marshlands skulk . . . He might have grown up near my family."

I scowled at him. "It was more than that. He knew you."

Siffrin shook his head and I caught a flash of his white bib. "I don't like these wild accusations. Have you forgotten who *saved* you from the Taken?" His fangs glinted in the low light. "I know you're upset, but watch what you say. I won't stand here and be insulted after everything I've done for you."

I gritted my teeth. He wasn't about to divert me with his false indignation. "Tarr *knew* you."

Siffrin flicked his tail. "Maybe the skulk have been speaking with their master . . . The Mage might have recognized me."

"Speaking how exactly? I thought you said that he lived in the Deep Forest, far away from here."

"He does."

My head was thumping as I struggled to understand. "And why would the Mage recognize you? You've never met him, have you? Never been part of his skulk?"

Siffrin's eyes slid away from mine. "I'm loyal to the Elders."

He hadn't answered my question. Beneath his rain-slicked coat, I could make out the reddish-brown grooves. They unfurled across the top of his foreleg like the broken petals of a ghoulish rose. Mist expanded along the deathway as the gray light of dawn lit its curling tendrils. "That scar on your foreleg . . . Who did that?"

Siffrin dropped his head, his shoulders stooped. He half turned instinctively, disguising his old injury. "Leave it, will you?"

My voice exploded in a gekker. "Tell me!"

He paused for a few beats as rain tumbled onto his fur and ran down his paws. I was holding my breath, the hairs flexing along my hackles. Finally, Siffrin lifted his head. I knew then, saw it before he said the words.

"The Mage did it. Are you happy now?"

I backed away from him, disoriented. Everything that had once seemed certain had turned to dust and air. I had grown to trust the red-furred fox, but all along he had lied about what he knew; lied about what he'd seen.

Lied about who he was.

Siffrin shook his wet fur. "Things are complicated, much more than you know. But believe me, Isla, I'm still the best friend you've got—I'm your only chance of finding Pirie."

"I don't need your help. You deceived me! You let me believe that my family was still alive." My voice began rising sharply again and I swallowed. My whiskers quivered and my flanks were heaving.

"This is bigger than you, cub. Don't you get that? There's more at stake here than a few urban foxes!"

"Those 'urban foxes' are all I've got! All I had . . ." My voice splintered and I dropped my gaze.

"I know," said Siffrin more softly. "I didn't mean . . . If you let me explain, I promise I'll never keep secrets from you again."

"You *promise?*" I spluttered. "What does a promise mean from a liar?"

The red fox winced, his large eyes full of sadness.

Good, I thought. *Let him suffer—it's less than a whisker of the pain I feel.* The slither of acid had expanded, hardened, was tearing through my throat like claws. "I don't want anything to do with you, the Elders, or anyone else. I'll find my brother on my own." I spun around on stumbling paws and started along the bank of the deathway, splashing through puddles as I picked up speed.

"Don't be a fool! The Graylands are dangerous!" he called after me.

I wheeled around with fangs bared. "I know they're dangerous! You can't trust *anyone*." I started to run. I could hardly see where I was going as I pounded over graystone, blinded by rain, by anger and grief.

"Please wait, I'm sorry!" Siffrin called, but I ignored him. As I cut across the deathway, his voice shrilled through the mist: "Isla, look out!"

A glance over my shoulder at the mangler's eyes. It screeched as I leaped into its path.

16

I darted across the deathway and crashed into the bank with a thud. Stunned, I shook my head. The borders of the bank were melding and blurring. I blinked and tried to rise onto my paws, but I slipped in a puddle, my body shuddering. Rain tumbled over my fur, sank into my ears, drenched my thoughts. I stared ahead blankly. Over the vague contours of graystone, I pictured Pirie running loops around the wildway, searching for the creature with the beautiful voice.

I squeezed my eyes shut. I was only faintly aware that the mangler had growled to a halt.

"Isla! What's wrong? Are you hurt? Get out of here! It's the snatchers!"

With an effort I opened my eyes and tried to focus. I twisted my head back to the deathway. The mangler was large and white with a short, angry snout. Its eyes still glared at me, dazzling my vision. I tried to tense and rise to my paws, my back legs scrambling beneath me. A furless was striding toward me, clutching a long shiny stick with a hoop at the end. His forepaws were huge and rubbery.

Siffrin was rushing up and down the bank as the furless drew closer. "Get away from her!" he barked, curling back his lips and throwing down his paws, then twisting out of reach with his back arched. The furless thrust the stick toward him, slamming it hard on the graystone as Siffrin dodged. From the edge of my vision I took in the quick, sharp movements, like rats' feet skittering over walls. But at the center of my vision was a lazy gust of mist—a fine, fuzzy rain that slowed everything down. The mangler's white eyes shone on the deathway; sticks seesawed over the spy hole above them and wiped away the rain.

The lumbering furless drew toward me.

I heard Siffrin's voice through a haze: "Why don't you run?"

A flare of hatred exploded inside me. *Deceitful fox.* I strained my back legs, but I couldn't rise. I stayed collapsed in the puddle, like a mound of earth. Through the stagnant filth I smelled a hint of the wildway. Bark, petals . . . the spicy soil. Were birds twittering in the sky above me? Was the sun bursting over the dew-touched grass? My eyelids were heavy as I sank deeper into the water, willing myself to another place.

I felt a sharp pain as a noose closed around my neck. I was dragged along the deathway at the end of the shiny stick. Siffrin danced around me, risking snaps at the furless's legs. The furless barked and kicked at him as he yanked me over the graystone. He dangled me by the neck and thrust me into the back of the mangler. I saw bars against the spy hole, fine railings that crisscrossed in both directions. They floated and doubled under my weary gaze, leaping in and out of focus.

The furless was going after Siffrin, raising his shiny stick. Siffrin ducked and snapped, and the furless barked in frustration. As the red-furred fox sprang out of reach, the furless slammed the stick on the ground and stomped toward the front of the mangler.

I gazed blankly beyond the railings. Siffrin was gekkering wildly, throwing his forepaws up on the spy hole. The beast rumbled to life, jerking forward abruptly. I clung to the mesh floor, which bit my paw pads. Siffrin fell back, rolled to his paws, and started to run. I saw him chasing the mangler, gritting his teeth with effort. He followed it along the deathway, yelping my name. As the mangler picked up speed he faded from view, a blot of deep red on the murky horizon. I shut my eyes, allowing the wildway to enclose me. Pirie was prancing through the grass. I could see the top of his mottled tail as it flicked back and forth. I bounded toward him but he slipped out of reach, into a soft green light.

I curled up in a tight ball. Every joggle of the deathway rattled my limbs. I was out of the rain, but I still felt water washing over me.

Everything had changed since I'd left my den. Even the hard walls of the Snarl seemed to melt and grow vague in the tangle of my thoughts. Ma, Fa, and Greatma . . . During all the nights I had looked for them, they had already passed into a vast, unknowable silence. Sorrow gripped me and I trilled for them, soft peeping sounds from the back of my throat, calling like a newborn.

Siffrin had known, had witnessed the end of their brutal deaths. But he had let me believe they were still alive.

And the shameful truth.

I had let myself believe it.

My senses pattered around the mangler, distorted and confused. Shreds of fox scent; shades of dusk. There was nothing left that was certain or solid, nothing secure in this damaged world.

Pirie's face floated into the spy hole of my thoughts. The ginger and gray of his muzzle was almost close enough to touch. The black tips of his ears were slightly rotated. His amber eyes watched me thoughtfully, his cream bib fluttered with his rising breath.

I was dimly aware of a faint *ka-thump, ka-thump,* a sound that reached through the earth and the air. It murmured so softly that it tickled my ears. *Ka-thump, ka-thump*. He had reached the furless with the wings of stone. *Ka-thump, ka-thump*. He had passed through the deathway where it climbed uphill. *Ka-thump, ka-thump*. My whiskers tickled. My eyes flicked open as the mangler hit a bump. Was my brother reaching out to me, his heartbeat lacing with my own?

I blinked hard and focused on the crisscrossed wire. The blurring lines grew sharper as my mind became alert, like light piercing fog. Pirie *was* alive! He was trying to reach me with his thoughts. As the sun rose over the Great Snarl, Pirie was touched by the same radiance.

A surge of relief thundered through me, so powerful that I yowled. If we could harness gerra-sharm, if we bridged the spaces that divided us, we could be together again. I would call to him; I would find him. Hope rekindled the warmth inside me. My tail thumped the mesh and I jumped up, momentarily confused. The deathway glinted in the morning sun. The rain had finally stopped and light glanced off pools of water along the bank. I caught glimpses of furless, pigeons, squirrels, and a blackbird. I looked about me, taking in, as though for the first time, the wire that enclosed me.

Only then was I gripped by the realization of where I was. In a mangler, with the snatchers, hurtling to the place where foxes were taken and never seen again.

The mangler lurched along the deathway, chugging and growling. Occasionally it hit a bend and I rolled onto my side. My gut twisted. I was glad I hadn't eaten recently. I had the sensation that the mangler was rising, spinning its strange twirling paws in ascent. I tried to look out of the spy hole, but when the mangler stopped abruptly I smacked my snout on the wire. Drawing back and licking my nose, I searched for a way to escape.

On the other side of the space where I was enclosed, I could just make out the back of the furless. His face was fixed on the deathway ahead and he didn't glance back as I watched him. The inside of the mangler was smooth and hard, sharp-edged, like everything in the land of the furless. I could see no way out.

I focused on the memory of Pirie, which was scorched on the eye of my mind. His mottled fur, his thrashing tail. I sucked in a deep breath and started to wash my paws. The mangler was just a way that the snatchers transported foxes. I tried not to think about where . . . Eventually, it would have to rest. The furless would return to me. Then I would find a way out.

The mangler rose higher, turning sharp corners. I could feel it slowing down, crawling along the deathway, other manglers pressing in around it. After a while it broke free, leaping forward with an angry hoot. My ears flattened and I braced against the mesh. I felt it swing around another bend. It paused, still rumbling, as it started to creep backward into what looked like a great, dark den. Abruptly it came to a halt and fell silent.

The furless was stalking toward the back of the mangler, clenching his huge forepaws. I shuffled back against the mesh. My muscles tensed, preparing to bolt. The moment he opened the back of the mangler, I'd spring past him. I thought of the rat I had chased into the dog's yard. It had seemed so calm—had lulled me into thinking I could catch it. I took a deep breath and let my ears twist forward. Like the rat, I would look calm. The furless wouldn't guess I was about to run.

I heard a click at the back of the mangler and slid back onto my haunches. But when the doors flew open, the rows of wire remained where they were. The furless reached into the mangler and pulled. He lifted me out in a wire box—there was no way to escape. I could see graystone through the mesh base and feel the air drift across my fur. Strange smells assailed my senses and the hairs bristled along my neck. I forgot my promise to be like the rat as I scrambled backward against the wire, a snarl in my throat.

The furless started carrying me toward a building. Another furless greeted him—I heard them yipping to one another. The second furless poked a rubbery paw pad through the wire and I spat as I sprang at it, trying my best to sink in my teeth. The flesh was too solid; I couldn't get a grip. The furless drew back her paw and cackled in amusement.

The wire carrier swung as they carried me into the building. The odors inside were much stronger. The first to hit me was a sharp, acidic smell that coated the white passageway. Beneath it I sensed the odor of foxes, but I had never known so many confined in such a small space. The stench was unbearable, like dozens of creatures fused together, airless, breathless.

Filth, decay, and something else.

The smell of fear.

It singed my nostrils. I could feel it clawing urgently at my throat as the furless carried me along the passageway. I bit down hard, fighting the panic that was flooding my thoughts. My body started trembling and I stifled a cry. As we turned along another passageway, I could hear the yelps and squeals of trapped foxes, and I grew rigid with the scent of their terror.

What is this place?

I heard the scratching of paws and occasional gekkers, but most of the creatures were strangely quiet. I growled and clutched the mesh base of the box, screaming at the furless to let me out, but both of them ignored me. Waves of bitterness rose in my throat. I couldn't believe this was happening to me: I had been warned about the snatchers since birth.

Sorrow had bewildered me, eroding my instincts and aware-ness. I had allowed myself to be caught.

As we turned into the room, I gave a panicked cry. There were walls of cages on either side, much smaller than those at the beast dens. Some seemed to be empty. The rest were filled with terrified foxes who cowered as the furless approached. Most dipped their eyes submissively. A gray male gave a yelp and buried himself against the far wall of his cage. In the next cage, there was a fox so ravaged by ill-ness that he barely had any fur on his skinny body. He didn't look up as I was carried past.

The next few cages were empty. Further along, a ginger female made a sudden move in my direction. Her amber eyes were wild. "Have you seen my cubs?" She eased against the wire of her cage, ignoring the furless. Her gaze was fixed on me. "The snatchers stole my cubs . . . They take the young ones first." There was a mournful wail from a nearby cage and the vixen lowered her voice. "He lost his cubs too . . ." She pressed her nose against the wire. "They took mine, born only yesterday. Four males, their eyes still shut. Have you seen them?"

I ran my tongue over my muzzle. "No," I mouthed, with-out a voice.

"Four males," she repeated. "Their eyes still shut. Only new to this world. Their coats were dark, not bright like yours." As the furless carried me further into the room the vixen craned her head after me, shuffling her forepaws on the wire. "Can you help me?" she whispered urgently. I couldn't see her anymore and I slumped back on the mesh, overwhelmed by the haunted faces beyond the wire. I heard the vixen's voice rising to a panicked howl. "Have you seen my cubs? There were four of them. The snatchers took them!"

The mournful wail rose again from another cage, and the room exploded into whines and gekkers.

The furless barked angrily and the foxes quieted down, cringing against the backs of their cages. They watched with only the odd mewl or whine as I was carried toward a yellow door, opposite the one where I'd entered. The furless paused in front of it, clucking to one another. I noticed a shabby old fox in a nearby cage, squinting at me through eyes clogged with grit. A stench hung around her, like sour milk . . . With a start, I recognized the sick old vixen—the one I had approached in a wildway the night my family disappeared.

You come. You ask for Pirie. You go. You come. When will you leave me alone?

"Why are you here?" she rasped.

I wasn't sure what she meant. Why was any fox here? "The snatchers caught me . . ." I murmured. "They put me in their mangler."

The vixen's face was contorted with pity and contempt. Did she remember me? I couldn't be sure. "I know that," she sniped. "But why let them catch you? You are young . . . You should have run away."

One of the furless was tampering with the top of the wire carrier, and I took in his clumsy, rubbery paws with alarm. I didn't know how to answer the vixen, or even if she expected a response. She was right—I should have run. I shouldn't be here. My eyes trailed over the cages. *No fox should be here.*

"What happens now?" I asked.

The old fox pushed her head closer to the wire of her cage. "What do you think? They round us up because we're vermin to them. Yesterday every cage in this room was full. Today . . ."

A chill ran through me as I took in the empty cages between the foxes.

"The rats they kill on the spot. The cats and dogs they keep elsewhere. Furless sometimes take the young ones home . . . but the old ones end up like us." The vixen nodded toward the yellow door. "One by one, the furless empty the cages and take them through there. The furless return, but the foxes don't come out." Her voice dropped to a crackle. "They took that vixen's newborns. I saw it. I hope they take her too, whining for them. The loss has driven her mad."

I could hardly breathe. The sour smell singed my senses. Panic stalked me. I started spinning in the wire box, whipping my eyes around the room.

"There's no use fighting," the old fox told me. "You may as well be patient. They start with the foxes who arrived first and work their way through the room." Her splayed ears quivered as her gaze moved over my shoulder. "The cages are already half-empty. It won't be a long wait . . ."

I spun around in time to see one of the furless draw a cage door open opposite the old vixen. The acid smell pricked my nose as the other furless unfastened the top of my box and slipped in his huge, rubbery paw. I fought wildly, ducking and flailing my legs, but as the paw clamped around my neck I fell still.

17

I had to run; I needed to fight. But the grip around my neck left me paralyzed. My body was limp as the furless lifted me out of the mesh box and tossed me into the cage. Released from his hold, I leaped to my paws, but the wire door had already snapped shut.

The wailing fox raised his voice in despair. Most of the others were mewling quietly, lost in their own miseries. Fighting the panic that tore through me, I worked my paws at the door. My claws skidded off the wire and the male furless snorted as he backed away. He and the other furless approached a cage on the opposite side of the room, two down from the old vixen. I hadn't noticed a fox in there before, but now I spotted a long gray paw. I stopped fighting with the wire and shuffled along the edge of my cage, trying to see around the backs of the furless. I could make out the fox's slim flank, ginger dappled with gray. There was a wound near the top of the foreleg that looked like it had already healed, perhaps some time ago: a series of reddish-brown lesions in the shape of a rose.

My heart flipped and I pressed closer.

You belong to him . . . We have seen the mark.

But it wasn't Siffrin. The legs were skinny with jutting bones. As the furless shifted, I caught sight of a dark gray face with a long, pointed muzzle.

"Tarr!" I yipped in surprise, and he turned to look at me. He couldn't reach me through the wire cages—he didn't even try. He stared without twitching a muscle. Beneath the bright lights, his eyes looked much redder. Even from this distance, I could just make out a cracked network of veins across their shiny surfaces. Gunk caked his eyelashes. Sallow froth clung to the corners of his mouth and he did not lick it away. Foxes yipped and mewled around him but Tarr did not seem to notice them. I frowned, craning closer to the wire. There was a lack of awareness about his whiskers. They should have been flexing and shifting, betraying the quick movement of his thoughts, but they were strangely still.

The Taken . . .

Of what Siffrin had told me, this at least must be true—I could see it plainly as I searched Tarr's face. His will had been stolen. He stared at me intently, and the black centers of his eyes seemed to expand and pulse red. A shiver ran through me. I flinched away from the wire, as though he could reach me with that chilling gaze. Siffrin was different; he seemed more alert—more *alive*—and yet I'd seen the mark on his foreleg.

My thoughts jumped to the Mage, the strange fox who dwelled in the Darklands, bending foxcraft to his own ends, but I yanked them back to the brightly lit room. I had to focus on my own survival if I was going to make it out of this place. My whiskers trembled and I saw Pirie playing in the wildway, a vision of warmth in the starkness of the snatchers' den.

Tarr was still watching me with those bloodshot eyes. I wondered what he was thinking—whether he was even capable of thought. Who had he been before the Mage had found him? It was impossible to imagine.

"What does Karka want with Pirie?" I yelped suddenly.

My cry unnerved the foxes around me. Yips and shrieks erupted from the cages and the male furless turned, raising his rubbery paw at me. But Tarr's face registered no response to my question. Slowly his jaw loosened. "Pirie?" he echoed.

I backed further away from the wire, disconcerted by his vacant stare. I watched as the two furless fiddled with the outside of his cage. They pulled the door open and closed a steely hook around Tarr's neck. He didn't struggle. They bundled him into a mesh carrier like the one they'd used to lock me in the mangler. Tarr held my gaze as the furless lifted him past me, toward the yellow door.

As the door slammed shut behind them, a volley of cries filled the brightly lit room. A new wave of panic coursed through the trapped foxes, whimpers of pity and horror.

The old vixen cringed against the wall. "Another one taken to be killed," she clicked sadly.

How could I tell her he was dead already?

My eyes roved over the cage. There was no way to escape, not when the door was shut. I would have to get out when the furless came to open it—that was my only chance. I thought of how they approached in twos, with strange ropes and sticks. I pressed my muzzle against the wire. There were no spy holes. Was the door leading into the room wedged open? I thought so. If it was closed, I would be trapped for good. But I still had to find a way out of the cage.

I remembered the mouse in the dark alley of the deathway, and the furless along the bank who walked by without seeing.

The yellow door swung open and the male furless strode out. He passed the cages without looking at any of the foxes, though I heard the fearful shuffles of their paws against the mesh floor as they shrank away from him. The furless disappeared from sight and I pressed my ear against the wire, listening intently. I didn't hear the slam or click of a door—

it seemed to be left open, as I'd suspected. A kernel of hope unfurled inside me. There was a dish of water in my cage and a small bowl of dry meat. Despite the churning sickness in my belly and the smell of filth that surrounded me, I forced myself to eat and drink. I would need energy for what I was planning.

I settled against the side of the cage and watched silently. As time crept on, two more foxes were brought into the room. Others, who had been there longer, were dragged in turn into a wire carrier and taken through the yellow door. None returned.

I lowered my head onto my paws with a long, sad breath. My tail drew around my flank as I tried to guess whether the morning had passed yet. Pirie always teased me for being impatient. So had Siffrin. My jaw tensed when I remembered the red-furred fox. What did he know?

Watch! Wait! Listen!

Two furless strode into the room to squeals of panic. I couldn't be sure they were the same ones as before. They made for the cages by the yellow door, and my heart started thumping, but instead of me, they turned to the old vixen. They grappled her out and bundled her through the door without even bothering to thrust her in a wire carrier. She gurgled in distress and I sank my head beneath my forepaws.

The yellow door closed again.

As the day wore on, my mind drifted to the Elders, the wise, mysterious keepers of foxlore who met at a raised shaft of rock in the Wildlands. I remembered what Siffrin had said before I ran from him in the rain, that Greatma seemed to know some foxcraft. Perhaps these arts had always been used by urban foxes—understood, but never named. Had Greatma heard about the Elders?

If only I could ask her . . .

A pitiful mewl escaped my throat and I wrapped my tail tighter around my flank. When I shut my eyes I saw the dark contours of the Snarl, the long stretches of the deathway I had walked in search of my family. My tail fell limp when my thoughts returned to Siffrin. The pain of his betrayal bit through my fur. That untrustworthy, arrogant fox. Stalking me in wa'akkir, approaching me first as a dog, then as myself . . . Yet I envied him his foxcraft. I longed to shape-shift into someone else—a stronger creature with deadly teeth. No one would touch me if I was large and fierce, like the black dog in the redstone yard.

My ears flicked back and I opened my eyes. A memory played at the back of my mind. Something about a lost fox . . . I stared at the wire door, though I scarcely saw it. Instead I pictured that red-furred face, his bronze eyes sparkling as he recited something Jana had told him:

A fox is lost to the Elders, beyond the fur and sinew of the greatest of Canista's cubs.

220

I felt a fresh tingle of excitement, and that curious suspicion that the fox was Pirie. But who was the greatest of Canista's cubs? Did "greatest" mean the fiercest, the cleverest, or simply the largest? Where would I begin to look?

I became aware that the room had grown quiet. I pricked my ears, training my attention on the space around me. I probed the stale air, tracing the contours of warmth and breath. There were only two more foxes left in the cages—the ones who had been brought in after me. One by one, the others had been carried through the yellow door. I jumped to my paws. Every hair on my body was awake. I could hear the click of furless steps just outside the room. Two sets, drawing closer. I swallowed down a knot of dread and gathered in my breath.

Ka-thump, ka-thump. My heart was racing.

Calm, I begged it, reaching for the deep silence that slept in all things—in the furthest reaches of the sky, in the belly of the earth, *kaa-thump, kaa-thump.*

Feeling more in control, I took a deep breath, my mind tripping over the chant as I prowled to the edge of the cage.

What was seen is unseen; what was sensed becomes senseless.

I hunched against the mesh, holding my breath.

What was bone is bending; what was fur is air.

The furless were drawing closer. I could sense their milky scent through the wire door. A gleam rose where they stood, but around them the world became cloaked in darkness. They seemed to pause uncertainly, to abandon the cage and return. Through the sticky pitch of my slimmer, I could hear them barking and sense their confusion as they peered inside the cage once more to find it empty. Then I caught another sound—of metal grazing wire; of the cage door swinging open.

As it swayed I saw the wire gleam, and I launched myself with all my might. My back legs skimmed a furless paw and I heard a yip of surprise overhead. I did not turn around.

What was seen is unseen; what was sensed becomes senseless.

I trod between the cages as slowly as I dared, forcing myself not to bolt till I was out of the room. I did not look up at the two caged foxes—could not even bear to think about them, waiting for their journey through the yellow door.

Out in the passageway, I gasped for breath, and the walls grew solid around me. I risked a glance over my shoulder and saw the furless pointing. One started toward me with thumping strides.

For a beat, I glared at him with a hatred so sharp that it crackled through my flesh. Then I turned and started to run. I knew he couldn't catch me—without a mangler, a furless could not keep pace with a fox; he was a clumsy, stumbling creature. I darted down the passageway, far ahead, drawing in great gulps of air. I snatched in a mouthful, a hint of a breeze; with a flicking ear I caught the growl of the deathway. The entrance to the den was two huge, pinned-back doors. I leaped through them with the furless far behind and slipped between parked white manglers. I knew that the furless wouldn't reach the doors till I was out on the death-way, jogging against the shadows of walls, hopping across the bank and weaving into wildways.

In my moment of darkness the furless had caught me. I vowed I would never let it happen again.

The sun was drifting low over the Great Snarl when I finally paused to regain my breath. I looked around me. The death-way plunged at a steep angle, spiraling down into the gloom. Turning around, I saw a grass bank overhanging the Snarl, a pinnacle that jutted above the streets. I trotted up some deserted steps, my whiskers bristling. The grass bank looked familiar.

My ears were twisting, my whiskers a whir of movement. I thought I heard the softest shuffle of paws and I jumped, my eyes scanning the redstone walls. A cat sauntered above me, along the top of a wall. She meowed plaintively and sprang off the far side. I could hear groups of furless yelping to each other below me on the deathway.

As I started to relax, I turned back to the towering grass bank. I had been here before . . . It was the corner of the large, neat wildway that hung over the Snarl—the one I'd reached on my first night alone. My ears pricked and I paused, drinking in my environment. I remembered the rows of fences and the beast dens with their peculiar smells.

A fox is lost to the Elders, beyond the fur and sinew of the greatest of Canista's cubs.

My tail was thrashing. Someone had taken my brother prisoner. It had to be true—what else could Jana's words have meant? I could picture Pirie's face, bright and vivid. The white tip of his mottled tail was almost in reach.

He wasn't with Karka—if he were, she wouldn't be looking for him. The "greatest of Canista's cubs" was the key to my brother's disappearance.

I remembered the beast with the yellow eyes, and the fur that fell about him like a knotted mane. Was Pirie trapped behind the bars of his enclosure, or by some savage art I could not understand?

The greatest of Canista's cubs . . .

Who could be greater than the wolf?

18

The wind had dropped. Even on the ridge, high over the Great Snarl, the air was mild. Clouds drifted out of eyeshot and a cool yellow sun hung over the sky. Down below coursed the endless tributaries of the deathway, woven in rings through the land of the furless. I felt like I had crossed every one of them since I'd left my family's den, only to return to this place of strange scents. I frowned, leaning over the pinnacle and trying to recognize each bend, each slab of graystone. The truth was I had only trod along a fraction of those paths—I wondered if anyone, any fox, any furless, had ever walked them all.

I edged along the wildway that sprawled over the hill. Across the cropped grass and neat flowerbeds, beyond the tall trees and colorful shrubs, were the beast dens encircled by bars. My heart skipped at the thought of Pirie, and my tail thumped the earth. But I had to wait. Groups of furless were milling in front of the building.

I slipped behind a tree and watched as they dispersed toward a flat graystone yard where manglers reclined in neat rows. The furless filed into the yard and climbed inside manglers, which promptly rumbled to life, stalking over the graystone and out of sight.

I scanned the beast dens. The outer fence caught the late sun, taking on a silvery gleam. One of the large doors beneath the arch was pinned back. More furless, mostly cubs, were streaming out of the open door and winding toward the manglers. A young male and female cackled and skipped behind two adults. With a long sigh, I sank onto my belly. I groomed my paws as I watched from behind the tree. Fewer furless were leaving through the door. Soon most of the manglers had pulled away. When it finally seemed quiet, I rose and started across the wildway toward the first set of bars.

As I drew closer to the archway, I heard the shuffle of steps. I scrambled back, diving behind some shrubs. A furless appeared, gazing through the open door. She drew it closed and I heard the clank of metal. My fur prickled. *Cages within cages.* I waited a little longer before creeping out from the shrub and sloping toward the bars. Slipping my muzzle between them, I could see the furless padding along the circular walkway around the dens.

I began to follow.

As I wandered along the inside, my nose was assaulted by smells and I was overwhelmed by the clamor of creatures: whines, snarls, clacks, hoots . . . I froze in my tracks, my whiskers pulsing frantically, my ears flipping forward and backward. I had forgotten how it felt, this onslaught to the senses, the many unknown creatures housed alongside each other.

The soft fur inside my ears was trembling like grass in the wind. On my previous visit it had been quieter, almost eerily silent—but that had been at night, when many beasts slept.

I took several shallow breaths. Feeling a little calmer, I started progressing along the bars again, tracking the furless from a safe distance. As I trod, I peered through the other fence—the low, widely spaced bars that circled the dens. I caught a glimpse of shimmering plumage. My paws faltered on the graystone. I wondered if the wolf was still in the same den. With a wrinkle of anxiety, I realized that he might have been moved. How long were creatures locked in the beast dens? I remembered the yellow door: the snatchers held foxes for less than a day.

Sadness crept along my tail, traveled up my back,

threatened to overwhelm me. I shrugged it off with a stiff shake. I would not allow myself to grieve for those foxes. I couldn't grieve for anyone.

I ran my tongue over my whiskers, squinting at the closest den. I could see a large pool and smell oily skin. I couldn't make out what dwelled inside, but it seemed as though the creature had been there for some time. I thought of the furless who'd been milling at the entrance to the beast dens. I pictured them treading along the bars, pointing and staring at the cages. Did it give them pleasure to see other creatures trapped?

Up ahead, the furless paused. Jangling some metal sticks, she eased open a door in the low fence and passed through, clicking it shut behind her. At the side of the fence, she gathered pawfuls of long grass and leaves, making for the nearest den. I slunk closer. I saw one of the furless's hind paws stamp onto a raised bar in front of the den. The bars swung outward, creating another door. The furless entered and dropped the grass and leaves on the ground, yipping to the creature inside. A long shadow crossed the den. An impossibly tall beast with a neck that extended further than a fox's entire body was gazing beyond the furless. Its coat was beige with splotches the color of earth. It watched me with large brown eyes. After a moment it lowered its strange, narrow head and started to munch at the foliage in a calm, untroubled way.

The furless backed out of the den and pumped the bar on the ground with her back paw. The door clanked shut again. She moved to the next den, lifting up a large trough and thumping her back paw on another raised bar. Again, she set down some food—this time, I couldn't make out what—and a lumbering, black-and-white striped beast approached furtively, clip-clopping toward the trough as the furless backed out of the den.

I looked about. Through the bars of the furthest fence, a red sun was setting. My interest in the furless vanished—all that mattered was that she was busy, that she hadn't noticed me. I had to find the wolf.

I proceeded in the other direction, circling the dens at a safe distance, keeping behind the low bars. Another furless was moving along the dens, but this time, instead of stepping on the raised bar and going inside, he threw hunks of meat through a flap in the wall.

So there were some creatures that even the furless were scared of. The thought gave me a thrill.

I remembered the strength and size of the wolf. I pictured teeth that could shatter bone. The furless were right to be afraid.

How would I find Pirie? If he was trapped in the wolf's den or by the beast's enchantment, how could I hope to free him?

Fox-ka! Conniving, crafty wretch!

That's what he'd said on our first encounter. A silvery resolve ran through my pelt. I would not creep; I would not try to trick him. I would confront the wolf—I would *demand* to see my brother.

But as I passed through the low bars and stalked toward the front of the wolf's cage, my confidence faltered. I could smell him, the great beast, the heavy tang of his grizzled coat. Fear crackled along my whiskers, mingling with wisps of hope. I remembered the light that glowed inside me, the strange warmth I'd felt after maa-sharm. I took a deep breath.

I stepped in front of the den, gulping down the wolf's pungent musk. The stench of meat struck me as my eyes rested on a hunk of bloody flesh on the ground inside the cage. There was a raised bar by the door, and I backed away from it. I lowered my head, ears flat, scanning the darkness of the den. I recognized the patch of grassy earth, the shrubs, and the small pond.

"Fox-ka."

My fur rose in spikes along my back. I caught the gleam of his yellow eyes. Despite the tall bars that divided us, I couldn't help shrinking away.

I could scarcely make him out—he was a dark outline in the shadows, under what looked like a canopy of branches. The red sky cast its haunting light across his den, adding a blood-tinged flicker to his shaggy pelt.

"What are you doing here?" he rasped. "Searching for rats?"

"I'm—" My voice cracked like splitting bark. I cleared my throat and tried again. "I'm here for my brother, Pirie. I want you to tell me where he is."

The wolf took a step forward. The pointed ears twisted as his shaggy head came into view. My body was braced, my back arching instinctively.

He towered over me. "Why should I know where your brother is?" he snarled with contempt. "Little thief, don't you learn? I care no more for your kind than for a flea."

I bristled, my tail stiffening. "I haven't come here for your insults, *Wolf*."

"You've grown braver, Fox-ka—at least with a set of bars dividing us. Why don't you come in here, and we'll talk more?"

I glimpsed the graystone path around the bars, the two rows of fences beyond, and the distant hum of red.

"I'm fine where I am."

With another step forward on his thumping paws, the wolf emerged from the shadows. His fur was burnished by the setting sun. His yellow eyes looked sunken, like brightglobes hemmed by stormy skies. A new leanness around his flanks only emphasized his lofty height. Beneath his knotted fur, I could make out the bend and brace of his bones.

My ears were flat behind me, the air squeezing tight around my chest, but I met the wolf's yellow gaze. "A fox is lost to the Elders, beyond the fur and sinew of the greatest of Canista's cubs."

The wolf's muzzle tightened. "What is this, Fox-ka?" His amusement was cooling. His ears twitched impatiently. I read his face for signs but found none.

I swallowed and held his gaze, recalling Siffrin's story about Dog, Wolf, and Fox. "Are you not the greatest of Canista's cubs? You're the largest."

The wolf looked beyond me, through the bars to the red twilight. I turned for a moment, trying to see what he was staring at. The beast dens had quieted. There was no sign of the furless now, just the silence of dusk and the hum of the Snarl down below. The red sunset was trailing a golden brush. A twist of clouds sank with it, like the white tip of a fox's tail. Rising above the diminishing light was a full moon on an indigo sky.

I glanced back to the wolf. "If you help me, I can get you out of here. I know how the doors work."

His eyes flicked to me for a moment. "I do not believe you, Fox-ka. If it were that simple, we would all be loose in the Snarl. Not that every beast here longs for freedom. Some aspire to nothing greater than regular food and a warm bed." He shuddered, his gaze sliding back to the moon.

"I do know how to do it," I insisted. "I watched the furless."

"Crafty fox. It doesn't matter anyway. I do not make deals with rat munchers."

My tail stiffened. Ignorant, superior creature. Heat gathered at my muzzle. "Don't you *want* to be free?"

He raised his long snout, tilting his head. His knotted coat looked filthy, with clumps of beige fur beneath his chin, but his voice was strong and proud. "What is freedom without honor?"

I could hardly believe what I was hearing. "Freedom is the sun on your whiskers, and finding your own food, sleeping where you choose, not answering to anyone!" *Freedom,* I thought, *was not to be haunted by the cries of others; not to be caged; not to quake in terror of the yellow door.*

"A creature that has shunned loyalty could never understand. You don't even hunt."

My voice rose into a gekker. "I caught some mice two nights ago!" I glowered, but the wolf still stared beyond me, to the moon.

"To run as a Bishar—that's what it means to truly hunt," he snarled. "To sprint across the frozen realms, a hundred paws pounding the snow in time, with a blizzard at your face, the bite of frost in your throat, and the spirit of your ancestors urging you on." His great paws clenched and relaxed to an untold rhythm. "A single beast, a single heart, as the hooves of your quarry beat a path like thunder. To risk the stampede; to sacrifice yourself, so that the Bishar survives. Never dead. Never forgotten. Always alive in the howls of the living."

The fur rippled at the base of my ears, though there was no breeze on the still air.

A light had come to the wolf's eyes, the last twinkle of burnished gold as the sun sank beyond the horizon. "At first I howled for them every night, hoping I would hear their voices or feel the shiver of ice in my fur. I do not howl anymore." He dropped his head and began to turn. Slowly he padded away from me, to the darkness of his den. He hadn't touched the meat that the furless had left him.

"Wait!" I begged. "Please tell me what you know about Pirie. He is my brother. He is all I have."

The wolf paused, half turning his head, his long snout in profile. "You spoke of others. Your fa . . . your ma?"

My voice splintered. "They are dead."

The wolf didn't speak for a while. His tail was low, flitting slightly like a drifting leaf. "Tell me again about this fox you're seeking."

I cleared my throat. "A fox is lost to the Elders, beyond the fur and sinew of the greatest of Canista's cubs."

The wolf's tail flicked. "I cannot guess what that means. Who spoke such words? How do you know they refer to your brother?"

"It's a feeling," I said quietly. "An instinct." My voice faded. I knew how foolish I sounded. "The words were spoken by an Elder Fox. You probably haven't heard of the Elders, but . . ."

The wolf was moving again, into darkness, out of sight. "You have come to the wrong place," he muttered.

I watched him melt into the shadows. I willed him to come forward, but the den was still. Moving heavily on my paws, I turned to look beyond the bars toward the wildway. The last shimmer of sun had vanished. Only a faint radiance hung over the low-cropped grass. My chest felt crushed, my breath labored. Of course Pirie wasn't here. I had been deluding myself, letting hope blind me.

A wave of sadness crashed over me. I ached with longing. Ma, Fa, and Greatma . . . beyond the horizon, out of reach forever. Pirie lost to me, both of us destined to wander alone. My thoughts tumbled to Siffrin, growing muddled as I pictured the red-furred fox. He had protected me, or so it had seemed—but he had also deceived me. I no longer knew who he was, what he stood for, what he wanted from me. Yet I mourned the friend I'd thought I'd found.

I drew in a deep breath.

Trust no one but family, for a fox has no friends.

I had no family either. Except for Pirie.

I gazed at the moon that had held the wolf in its thrall. The world he'd described was so distant, unrecognizable from the Great Snarl.

A land of mist and ice.

A single beast, a single heart.

My eyes strayed from the moon to the pinpricks of gold in the darkening sky. Canista's Lights glittered, awaking the deep warmth inside me.

Pirie was treading briskly through a long tangle of grass. Not an image from the past, not the wildway by our patch, enclosed between jostling buildings. Where Pirie stepped, grasses expanded far ahead, slashed by the gleam of lakes. He licked his lips thirstily, but there was no time to stop. He had to keep moving.

With Canista's Lights prickling the back of my eyes, Pirie's image grew more vivid.

His ears rotated and his mouth opened. His mottled tail gave a small wag.

Isla, can you see me? I'm waiting for you.

My breath came in a rush, my tail thumping the gray-stone near the fence. Why had I thought that the wolf could help me? The great creature was wretched, broken—he scarcely seemed able to help himself. I looked across the bars, glanced into dens. Pirie was not here. He was somewhere lush and green, a space free of towering buildings. A thrilling thought: a place where the furless did not rule.

He was in the Wildlands.

Hope glittered in the air, touched my coat, bubbled inside me. I started to run, to slip between bars, to make for the wildway. Pirie was reaching for me, and I was reaching back. I paused, eyes closed, seeking out his face.

Pirie, I'm here—I will find you.

When I opened my eyes I heard a whimper from one of the dens. There were a couple of clucks. In a neighboring den I heard an anxious braying. Did these creatures have families far away, parents or brothers they would never see again?

I thought of the snatchers, and the foxes that waited to pass through the yellow door. I tried not to remember the two left in the cages when I'd run out. *I should have helped them. But how?* My tail curled around my flank and a pang of guilt ripped through me.

Canista's Lights beckoned me away from the Snarl, to a place where the grass grew long and lakes riddled the land. But still I hesitated, turning back to the dens. So many lonely creatures . . . My paws were propelling me, drawing me closer. I jogged along the inside of the bars and heard that pitiful braying again. I stopped in front of the creature's den. It was the large, black-and-white striped beast that had nervously approached as the furless gave it food. Its huge body smelled of straw and earth. I could hardly see its face, only the glint of its staring eye. I stalked nearer to the entrance of the den and it shied back—despite its great size, it was scared of me. I found the raised bar on the ground and pressed my forepaws against it. The bar didn't budge. I withdrew, cocking my head. Then I thrust both forepaws onto the bar, using as much force as possible. With a stiff creak, the bar dropped, and the door to the den eased open.

The striped beast peered through the door, its large round eyes roving over the darkness. Then it took a tentative step forward on narrow, clacking paws.

Encouraged, I fell back and started for the next den. The tall beast with the brown splotches was standing quite still by the entrance. Its thin tail hung limp and its eyes were closed. Did this peculiar creature sleep standing up? When I jumped on the raised bar, it opened its eyes with a start. With a grunt, it stretched its spindly legs and made for the exit.

I started running from den to den, stamping on the raised bars and releasing the creatures. All the time, I thought of the snatchers and the foxes who'd cowered in small wire cages. The enclosures in the beast dens weren't as bad; maybe the wolf was right—that some of the creatures did not yearn to leave. I guessed that others were too small to scale the low fence, or too broad to slip between the bars. Even those who got through would need to find a way around the outer fence.

At least they had a chance at freedom, something the snatchers never gave those foxes.

The beast dens were coming to life. As I ran between them, I heard hoots and howls, yelps and clacks. Looking behind me, I saw two birds with tail feathers longer than a fox's brush; I watched the striped, black-and-white creature leap the low fence with ease, cantering over the graystone. Green birds with red faces were soaring through the sky, darting and swooping into the night.

I slowed down. I had rounded back to the wolf's den. I felt him watching me from the darkness.

"What are you doing?" he growled, giving me a fright.

I hesitated. "I'm releasing some of the creatures. The ones I can reach . . . the ones who can escape."

"Why?" That deep, rumbling voice.

"Every creature has the right to be free."

"I hope you don't intend to release *me*," he rasped. "I won't take favors from a fox."

My whiskers bristled. "Perhaps you'll have no choice." I moved toward the raised bar.

I heard a scuffle of paws and saw a family of furry creatures, like cats with small round ears and long flat tails. They charged past me, scrambling through the bars. The beast dens were becoming raucous.

The wolf snarled over the whinnies and yelps. "You won't free me—you wouldn't dare. A wolf cannot tolerate a fox. I may be forced to kill you."

Fear shot along my back and I stiffened. "I don't think you'd do that."

I saw the gleam of his eyes. "Why not?"

"Because you spoke of honor. Killing me wouldn't be a very noble act. Even if you hate me, your own beliefs would prevent you." I paused over the bar. Though my gaze was still fixed on the wolf's den, I caught a scrabble of movement against the furthest bars. Had a group of beasts gathered there? What if they turned on me when I tried to escape? A chill ran through me, the sting of uncertainty.

The wolf didn't answer, but his yellow eyes glinted. I heard the click of his teeth as they met. I remembered his black lips peeling back, that his fangs were as long as a fox's paw.

You won't free me—you wouldn't dare.

A vision of the wolf's tongue beyond those jagged fangs. The delicate center that lived in all things. I had said every creature had a right to be free, but did I really believe that? What about those who would gladly kill me? What about beasts with yellow eyes and huge fangs?

I thought of Pirie and his mottled coat.

Of twisting grass and glistening lakes.

Of sunshine and petals.

Of twinkling lights.

My forepaws slammed down on the raised bar and the door to the wolf's den flew open.

19

I turned sharply and started along the bars, almost slamming into a couple of huge white birds that waddled on their flat hind paws. My ears twisted at a high-pitched chittering, and I looked up to see a furry creature hoisting itself over the low fence with its long, winding tail. The creature squawked at me, baring its sharp teeth. Its face was bald. It looked like a small furless, except for the colorful pelt over its body.

I didn't like its leering stare. I hurried passed the small creature, eager to get away from the beast dens now that the entrance to the wolf's enclosure was open. The noise was bewildering, a throbbing clamor of hoots, squeals, yips, and gurgles, of sounds I could not describe or understand. I cut through the wide bars of the low fence and glanced back. The door to the nearest den was open. Inside I spotted the

vast gray beast with the horn on his leathery snout—
the one who'd been asleep on my previous visit. Its small
eyes took in the chaos on the far side of the bars, and it held
back warily.

I heard a thump and swiveled around to see that
the striped, black-and-white creature had kicked open the
double doors of the far fence with its hard hooves. It burst
across the wildway with a whinny. The long-necked creature
with the brown splotches trotted behind it on legs like
branches. A screeching alarm cut through the air. It didn't
burble, it wasn't alive—it was static, a siren, like the howls
that rose from the Snarl. It was a signal to the furless: soon
they would arrive.

I stood on the grassy wildway, glancing back at the beast
dens. I saw the contours of creatures: round, skinny, loping,
striding . . . I turned back to the vista and Canista's Lights. I
had to find the path to the Wildlands, where Pirie was
bounding between lakes.

The stars were peaceful. The air was still as the commo-
tion erupted behind me. I skirted along the wildway. Siffrin
had said that the Wildlands began where the sun set, circling
east and west beneath the Snowlands. He had said a lot of
things . . . I pictured the light that had traveled, red-brushed
and burnished, over the furthest tip of the Snarl. I sensed
that in this, at least, he had spoken the truth. Reluctantly, I
rejoined the deathway. I knew I would have to walk it a while

longer, to follow it beyond the limits of the Graylands. I would be patient—I would persevere. Hope thrummed at the base of my ears.

With a sigh, I allowed the graystone to enclose me, walls rising on either side. A brightglobe fizzed up ahead. Around the bend, a mangler bleated.

There was a scuffle of paws close behind me. Was it a creature from the beast dens? I swung around, blinking into the darkness beyond the reaches of the brightglobes.

"Who is it?" I said cautiously, my fur prickling. In the distance, I saw creatures tumbling over the wildway and heard the shriek of the alarm. My ears pricked up. Slowly, I turned back toward the deathway.

Another step, another scuffle.

I stood a long time, searching the edges of the wildway. Whatever I'd heard wasn't moving anymore. But I sensed it was close, watching, waiting. My heart started thumping against my ribs. My brush swished over the graystone. In the distance, I heard the screech of a mangler and saw a furless running across the grass with forepaws flailing.

Slowly, I turned back to the bank of the deathway. A furtive pawstep. Another pause. At the pit of my stomach, I felt a germ of dread.

I swiveled my head, my ears twisting this way and that. A silhouette flitted over the graystone and a cackle exploded above me. I looked up to see a flock of green-and-red birds, lighting up the dreary deathway. When I lowered my eyes to the graystone, my heart shrieked with terror.

The round ears, the muscular frame . . . The single gray eye was unforgiving. When she blinked, the livid flesh in the other socket convulsed. I stumbled away from her, from the foxes that stepped from the shadows like ghosts.

Karka flashed her serrated teeth. "Where's the Darklands fox? Don't tell me he left you all alone."

I lapped at my muzzle. My throat was dry as dust. I flicked my eyes over the deathway ahead. I smelled a tang of acrid fur, of smoke and cinders. More foxes blocked the path before me, their faces grim. How had they found me, so far across the Snarl? I'd traveled in a mangler. They couldn't have tracked my scent.

An image pierced my memory: Tarr's blank stare from his cage in the snatchers' den. His whiskers were stiff and the centers of his eyes pulsed red. I remembered Siffrin's words as he begged for understanding: *Maybe the skulk have been speaking with their master . . .* At the time, I'd dismissed this as a desperate attempt to redeem himself, to distance himself from Karka and the others. Had the red-furred fox guessed right? Had someone else seen through Tarr's dead gaze, just as they had controlled his will?

"The Master wants the cub," she snarled. "Take her alive, if she can be trapped—but better to kill her than to let her run free."

Panic tore through my chest as the dead-eyed foxes stalked closer. Their voices rose in wailing snarls. Their tails were tense and straight as sticks. My eyes shot along the high walls. Every route, all escapes, were closed to me. I struggled to keep control of my terror, to find the deep strength I had harnessed in the snatchers' den.

"Where is Pirie?" I squealed.

Karka's lip curled with amusement. "Beyond your reach: you will never find him."

"It isn't true," I gasped, despite my fear. "I will search the whole earth if I have to."

"You're dreaming," she snarled. "You won't have the chance. Soon you will be like them." She tipped her muzzle at the blank-eyed foxes, who took another step toward me.

As Karka's skulk closed in, I remembered the green-and-red birds who had soared to freedom. I threw my voice to the windless sky. A cackle burst over the foxes' heads and they faltered, shying back in confusion. I strained to mimic another call, the mocking chittering of the creature that looked like a shrunken furless; then the clack of a bird; then the yowl of a beast. Staccato squeaks, yelps, and twitters. Sounds leaped to my mind from the beast dens and sprayed from my mouth in a clamorous blizzard.

To my amazement, the foxes started to turn, treading tight circles. Their hindquarters dropped and their muzzles rose in fear. They cringed from the sounds and backed into each other with high-pitched gekkers. Encouraged, I thrust my voice to all corners of the sky, a storm of sounds that rattled the night. I sucked in my breath and began to slimmer, slowly, slowly slinking between them.

"Idiots!" screeched Karka, slamming down a mighty paw. One of the foxes snapped out of his trance, but the others were whimpering, spinning, confused. Elated, I hissed like a furious cat and two of them started to run down the deathway.

Karka exploded with rage. "How dare you! Get back here, you cowards! Get back before I snap your necks!" She turned to me, her gaze full of vengeance. I felt it like a jolt to the chest. My breath burst from me and my karak faded, a dying cackle on the still night air.

Exhausted, I slumped onto the graystone. The slimmer and karak had sucked up my maa. The foxes dropped their heads, their hackles raised. They were closing in and I was powerless to stop them.

Karka started to chant: "I am the fur that ruffles your back. I am the twist and shake of your tail. Let me appear in the shape of your body: no one can tell; others will fear; dare not come near!"

I gaped, heart thundering, as Karka sprang into the air, her lips a mutter of snarls and growls.

Her body spun and she landed before me as the largest dog I had ever seen.

The dog's fur was as sharp as wire. Her eyes were as black as a midnight pool, and muscles rippled beneath her flesh. She squared up to me with white drool on her fangs.

I squeezed my eyes shut as she loomed above me. I couldn't allow her to take me alive. To live was to have my will snatched from my body—to be a thing without my own thoughts. I dragged myself over the graystone and girded my will deep within my chest. I heard the thump of Karka's paws as she approached.

A blood-curdling yowl and my eyes flew open. Two foxes were slumped on the ground beside me. A flower of blood unfurled on the graystone.

The Taken bled like any fox.

Shifting back into her own form, Karka wheeled around with a startled yelp. What had she seen that made her turn her back on me? What had killed the foxes that lay at my side? The other foxes squealed with terror, turning to break over the deathway.

Blinking wildly, I realized it was just me and Karka. The others had abandoned her, their terror sharp on the air.

A shadow moved over Karka's body.

And then I knew: we were not alone.

A growl rumbled from the belly of the earth. A beast appeared, with pointed ears and a white, shaggy pelt. He seemed even larger without bars between us.

The great wolf opened his jaws. Karka stayed frozen, held in his thrall. He sprang upon her and threw her down, fastening his deadly fangs around her neck. With a brutal snap he shook her and then dropped her, letting her head roll on the graystone.

She stared at him with her single gray eye. Would stare like that forever.

The wolf's maw was wet with blood as he lowered his gaze to look at me. And I blinked back: trapped between horror and admiration, between terror and hope. Was he about to kill me too?

Slowly the strain released at his muzzle, and I no longer saw the length of his teeth. His eyes fixed on me. "What is your name, Fox?"

I took a quick look across the deathway. It was quiet now beneath the hum of nearby manglers. Beyond the dead bodies of Karka and two of her skulk, I could make out movement on the wildway. The furless were locking up the beast dens, rounding up the last of the creatures. But some had gotten away: I remembered the green-and-red birds.

And the wolf. He had escaped after all.

"My name is Isla."

"Is that all?" he asked in surprise. "No pack name? No family allegiances?"

My ears flicked back. "Until I find my brother, I'm alone in the world."

The wolf watched me evenly. He started forward and I grimaced. But instead of setting on me, he gave a deep bow, stretching his forepaws before him and lowering his hindquarters, dipping his head against his chest.

"Well then, brave Isla," he said solemnly. "You can call me Farraclaw. I am a wolf of the Snowlands. You released me, despite my resistance, and I am in your debt."

I watched in silence as he rose to his great height, his fur cascading over his shoulders. "I bid you luck in finding your brother. No cub of Canista should be alone. I too shall seek the ones who know me by my heartbeat. I shall listen for them until their voices thunder from the skies. I will call for them until I am home." He threw back his head with an unearthly howl that shook the air. The hairs tingled all over my body. I shut my eyes, bolstered by the strength of the wolf's voice, which seemed to heal my fragile maa. When I opened my eyes, I felt restored. My mind was alert, my soul full of hope.

I looked for him, but the wolf had gone.

When I was very young, with eyes scarcely open and ears still floppy, I heard the beautiful call of an unknown creature. Its voice danced and spun in mysterious loops, brilliant like ice as a cold dawn broke. I was sure that the creature was as large as a fox to master such a powerful voice.

I had searched for it with Pirie by my side; I had listened for it from the night he'd vanished.

I finally found it as I left the land of the furless, on the branch of a tree near a guttering brightglobe, right on the edges of the Snarl. My tail drooped with disappointment: it was only a bird—a small, round creature with a red bib at its throat.

Pirie's voice in my head. *Why are you sad?*

I watched the ball of feathers as it flitted from the tree. "I thought I would see a powerful thing," I said to no one. "I thought it was something special."

My brother's voice was fading as the bird escaped from sight. *Perhaps it is,* he murmured, the slightest whisper on the breeze.

I paused, training my ears. I could no longer hear Pirie, but distantly I caught the call of the bird. My tail gave a wag as I drank in in its beautiful song.

First light was climbing over the Great Snarl. Far behind me, the brightglobes would be flickering into darkness as the sun rose over the murky sky. I wondered if Siffrin was still there, searching for me along shady alleyways. A flicker of regret caught my whiskers, and I shook it away. His deceit still burned deep in my belly. I was better off without him.

I had followed the deathway through the night, where the graystone broadened, then twisted, then lunged between grasses. Up ahead there were dappled green fields, edged by rolling hills and trees that grew higher than furless dens.

Somewhere out there was the Elder Rock, and places I only knew by their names: the Wildlands, the Snowlands, the Darklands.

And Pirie.

I didn't know where he was; I had no clue how I would reach him. But I knew that my brother was still alive. When I closed my eyes I saw him clearly, bounding through long grasses, raising his head above the morning mist. Perhaps Karka was right; I was dreaming if I thought I could find him in this great, mysterious world.

But dreams are the beginning.

☙ GLOSSARY ❧

FOXCRAFT

KARAKKING

Imitating the call of other creatures. The technique allows the fox to "throw" his or her voice, so it appears to come from elsewhere. Used to attract prey or confuse attackers.

SLIMMERING

Stilling the breath and the mind to create the illusion of invisibility. Prey and predators are temporarily disoriented. Used to avoid detection.

WA'AKKIR

Shape-shifting into another creature. Misuse of wa'akkir can lead to injury or death. Its practice is subject to ritual and rites that are closely guarded by the Elders.

MAA-SHARM

Maa is the energy and essence of all living things. Maa-sharm transfers maa from one fox to another. Used to heal frail or wounded foxes.

GERRA-SHARM

Gerra is the thinking center of living beings—the mind. Gerra-sharm allows foxes to share their thoughts. It is a rare foxcraft—a forgotten art—and can only be performed by foxes with an intense, intuitive bond.

⊰TERMS⊱

BISHAR

A mysterious title used by snow wolves to describe their packs. Little is known to foxes of these creatures or their ways.

BLACK FOX

The ultimate master of foxcraft. An honorary title bestowed on the wisest fox—there is only one Black Fox in any age, and he or she is traditionally an Elder.

CANISTA'S LIGHTS

A constellation of stars that are the basis of a fox's maa.

DEATHWAY

Also called the death river. These are roads, but to foxes it appears as the deadliest trap of the furless.

ELDERS

A secret society of foxes dedicated to keeping foxlore and foxcraft alive.

FOXCRAFT

Skills of cunning and guile known only to foxes. They are used in hunting or to elude the furless. Only gifted foxes will master the higher arts, such as wa'akkir.

FOXLORE

The fox's age-old struggle to survive the torments of the furless is captured in stories of resistance against all efforts to tame or destroy the fox. This lore distinguishes foxes from other cubs of Canista. Foxes understand dogs and wolves only in terms of their treachery. On one side, dogs are slaves to the furless; on the other, wolves are savages that howl to warlike gods. Foxes stand between them, answering to no one.

GERRA

The seeing, thinking center of living beings—the mind.

GLOAMING

The gloaming occurs between twilight and dawn on the longest and shortest days of the year. A time of great magic.

MAA

The energy and essence of all living things.

MALINTA

Malinta occurs twice a year, when day and night are of equal length. A time of magic.

MANGLERS

Cars. To foxes they appear as fast, growling predators with shining eyes.

⇥ PLACES ⇤

GRAYLANDS

The city. Also called the Great Snarl. Filled with manglers, dogs, and many other dangers.

WILDLANDS

The countryside, where many foxes live, including the Elders. Isla's fa is from here.

SNOWLANDS

The frigid northern realms where the snow wolves live, hunting in packs known as Bishars.

ACKNOWLEDGMENTS

I am grateful to the foxes of Myddelton Square, who have met my fascination with the confidence and grace of their species.

A growing skulk of fox enthusiasts has supported me in researching and writing this book: Trevor Williams and everyone at The Fox Project, who shared their insights, and introduced me to fox cubs; Kathryn Evans, who fortified me with soup and raspberries, and took me to meet foxes at Brent Lodge Bird & Wildlife Trust; and Priscilla Barrett, whose understanding of canid behavior has been invaluable.

I couldn't have found a more supportive editorial team in Zachary Clark, Abigail McAden, and Samantha Smith at Scholastic, whose passion for foxes matches my own.

Thank you to Team Fox at the Blair Partnership, including (but not limited to) Neil Blair, Liz Bonsor, Ellen Marsh, Jessica Maslen, and my incredible agent, Zoe King.

Thank you to Keren David, Tali Iserles, Naomi O'Higgins,

and Lee Weatherly for valuable observations on the manuscript; to Richard Mansell for ongoing advice; and to all of the Charlotte Street Group for writing camaraderie.

Thank you to Dganit Iserles for accepting my love of animals from the youngest age, and indulging my need to stroke cats, talk to dogs, and search for foxes.

Finally, I would like to show my appreciation to Peter Fraser and Arieh Iserles, who have always found time to listen to my fox-thoughts and have responded with wisdom and patience. You have been my steadfast oracles through this quest.

ABOUT THE AUTHOR

Inbali Iserles is an award-winning writer and an irrepressible animal lover. She is one of the team of authors behind the *New York Times* bestselling Survivors series, who write under the pseudonym of Erin Hunter. Her first book, *The Tygrine Cat*, won the 2008 Calderdale Children's Book of the Year Award in England. Together with its sequel, *The Tygrine Cat: On the Run*, it was listed among "50 Books Every Child Should Read" by the *Independent* newspaper.

Inbali attended Sussex and Cambridge Universities. For many years she lived in central London, where a fascination with urban foxes inspired her Foxcraft trilogy. She now lives in Cambridge, England, with her family, including her principal writing mascot, Michi, who looks like an Arctic fox and acts like a cat, but is in fact a dog.